P9-AOX-072

ALSO BY COURTNEY·ANGELA BRKIC

The Stone Fields

PICADOR

FARRAR, STRAUS AND GIROUX

NEW YORK

"On the page, nothing thwarts Brkic's fearless imagination. *Stillness* is her literary debut, and it is a remarkable one . . . . The writing . . . is eloquent beyond paraphrase."

—*Chicago Tribune*

"A striking collection that captures fully realized individuals braving the horrors of war."

—*The Oregonian* (Portland)

"Sterling stories . . . [an] indelibly empathic debut collection . . . Brkic's refined, surprising, and resonant stories encapsulate the truth about humankind's capacity for violence, selfishness, and altruism."

—*Booklist*

"Her strong, lean writing vividly details the wasteland through which her characters struggle as they try to hold onto shreds of their humanity. . . . The results are poignant and powerful."

—*Library Journal*

"*Stillness* manages the difficult fusion between a subject of substantive, brutal power and a literary style of unadorned grace. . . . Witness in and of itself cannot achieve the authentic leap of empathetic imagination that informs—that haunts—every sentence in this original and memorable debut collection."

—Stuart Dybek, author of *I Sailed with Magellan*

"Like Ondaatje, Courtney Brkic exhales a redemptive poetic quietude onto the page. The dead of Yugoslavia peer at us from behind her words."

—Tom Paine, author of *Scar Vegas*

"These marvelous stories full of sharp observations and touching moments show you more clearly and passionately what people go through in a war than most books of journalism do."

—Josip Novakovich, author of *Salvation and Other Disasters*

STRAND ANNEX

Stillness

AND OTHER STORIES

COURTNEY ANGELA BRKIC

STILLNESS. Copyright © 2003 by Courtney Angela Brkic. All rights reserved. Printed in the United States of America. No part of this book may be used or reproduced in any manner whatsoever without written permission except in the case of brief quotations embodied in critical articles or reviews. For information, address Picador, 175 Fifth Avenue, New York, N.Y. 10010.

www.picadorusa.com

Picador® is a U.S. registered trademark and is used by Farrar, Straus and Giroux under license from Pan Books Limited.

For information on Picador Reading Group Guides, as well as ordering, please contact the Trade Marketing department at St. Martin's Press.
Phone: 1-800-221-7945 extension 763
Fax: 212-677-7456
E-mail: trademarketing@stmartins.com

Designed by Gretchen Achilles

Library of Congress Cataloging-in-Publication Data

Brkic, Courtney Angela.
    Stillness and other stories / Courtney Angela Brkic.
        p. cm.
    ISBN 0-312-42256-3
    EAN 978-0312-42256-1
    1. Yugoslav War, 1991–1995—Fiction. 2. War stories, American. I. Title.

    PS3602.R535 S7 2003
    813'.6—dc21   2002029777

First published in the United States by Farrar, Straus and Giroux

First Picador Edition: August 2004

10 9 8 7 6 5 4 3 2 1

For my parents

Someone has simply stolen it all.

How else can we explain that not even Shadows remain?

—SINIŠA GLAVAŠEVIĆ, "PRIČA O GRADU"

Mother mine, my mother

One dream I dreamt

One dream I dreamt

That the war was over

—*from* "UNA NOCHE AL LUNAR,"

a Sephardic song from Sarajevo

Contents

Preface

Today is my birthday. I am twenty-four years old.

I am trying not to think about the waterlogged letters I translate, the names on the identity cards that I painstakingly transcribe. Only the pictures that we have recovered preoccupy me. The photographs sewn into a coat lining or tucked in a breast pocket have been erased by a year underground. By blood and by water. There is no way to discern what the photographs represent, even with words penciled on the backs: "The children and me." "Birthday, 1990." "On the coast." The writing has remained, the faces are gone.

The photographs are ghostly. They are pictures of white, foggy skies. From now on, when I have nightmares, I think the world will be painted in that color. My eyes strain to pick out some edge in the steam-colored surface, some feature from nothing, but I cannot. They are pictures of the dead.

There are few entries in the notebook I took to Bosnia in 1996. Examining it now, I notice the expanses of white paper that are broken only sporadically by my scrawl. The letters are like erratic and bloody footprints in the desert.

I had learned of forensic teams going to Bosnia a few weeks before that entry, and I applied to join them. My work as a field archaeologist in the United States had given me a skill for which there was a demand, and the irony of the situation was not lost on me. After a year of recording data on the refugee population in neighboring Croatia, I knew many women who had been going to bed every night for years without knowing the fates of their husbands and sons.

I had toughened myself in order to complete a year's worth of research, but at the end of it I would remember none of the statistics so carefully constructed from an onslaught of bleak words. Rather, I was incapable of forgetting an odd assortment of details: the ceremony one woman performed each night by placing a bowl and cup on the table for her missing son; the baby pictures carried in cracked leather wallets; the woman who had told me that after four years of sleeping alone she still slept on her side of the bed, keeping the adjoining space sacred for her husband should he return one day. My work with them convinced me that my presence at the exhumation of mass graves was more than appropriate. It was necessary.

And then there was my own family, which since the Second World War included a number of the missing. They were men whom I could picture in vivid detail but who had disappeared long before my birth. In a way, I prepared for Bosnia with a strange sense of justice. Words seemed ineffective to me. In Bosnia I could finally do something.

My Croatian Catholic blood did not make me a returning native daughter. I came to a Bosnian Moslem area that was foreign to me. My roots were in the south, in the rocky, harsh landscape of Herzegovina and the mountains of Dalmatia, and my accent was a strange amalgam of those speeches, thwarted by an American tongue.

But my father had grown up in Sarajevo, and that blood and that language differentiated me from the relief workers, UN personnel, and other foreigners who roamed the region in the summer of 1996. I occupied a sort of limbo, not wholly native and not wholly foreign. I came, too, with my own bitter memories of the war in neighboring Croatia, memories that included the ambivalence of outsiders.

In the morgue and on-site, I found letters and prayers in shirt pockets or rolled up with amulets inside tiny leather pouches that the dead had worn around their necks. The faded words were written in a language that I could understand, and I carried them in my head long after providing translations for the rest of the forsenic team.

In Bosnia, I performed a peculiar rescue of those already dead.

Meanwhile, the actual survivors of those years sat in refugee camps or walked on the roads as we sped past, kicking up clouds of dust and grit which made them appear ghostly as they receded in our rearview mirrors. Some were missing arms and legs, others had scars like maps that told harrowing stories of what they had witnessed. Still others had no marks, but were disintegrating from the inside. Their surviving children drew pictures on the backs of labels and scraps of paper, or with sharp sticks in the dirt, using small stones to show color: blood-red sky, blood-red sun, and small decapitated figures that cried and bled.

By the time I left Bosnia my dreams had become cloud-colored landscapes, light darkness in which I crouch and make myself as small as possible. I can hear other people breathing around me. I know them from some other time, but have forgotten their histories and names. Through that space their blood flies, warm and metallic. It coats my eyelashes and I blink in blind panic, in fury. I blink and waken. I drink in the air like water.

The stories are there like the most faithful of bedfellows.

They tell me: *We the living.*

NEW YORK, NOVEMBER 2001

Stillness

In the Jasmine Shade

ON THE LAST MORNING of that other life, the air had seemed sharp
as she awoke, as if she were looking through a lens designed to
bring everything into searing focus. There was none of the usual
grogginess that accompanied waking, nor did she turn and huddle
closer to her husband's warmth, hoping to regain the dream landscape from which she had just emerged. She could not remember
dreaming at all and lay with her eyes open wide.

Listening, she realized that the shelling and gunfire which had
torn the silence of the past several weeks had come to a halt. The
morning was conspicuous in its quiet, lending painful clarity to
details in the room which she would not ordinarily have noticed.

Wall and ceiling met in a crease that caused an ache in her chest, and she lowered her gaze to the pictures on the opposite wall and the books stacked on the heavy wooden armoire. Despite the lowered blinds, which made shadows cling to the floor and corners like a low-slung fog, she was able to read their titles.

Marko stirred beside her and she turned onto her side, watching as he became still again, his eyelashes like dark wings against the paleness of his face. *Marko*, she mouthed, watching his chest rise and fall. She held a hand in front of his face, near enough to feel a faint exhalation. Careful not to wake him, she closed her fingers like the petals of a flower over the warmth of his breath. *What's going to happen now?*

His eyes had opened in the half-light, as if aware that his wife's hand hovered over his face. His expression as he watched her was so somber that for a moment she tasted something like burning paper as a slow, sad fire rose in her throat.

But then he smiled, rolling her gently onto her back, and lowered his face to her ear. The scent of burning receded and she could feel the brush of his lips against her neck, moving to form the letters of her name. *Lejla*.

Yesterday's decision to spend the last night in their bed had come after weeks of sleeping on an old mattress in the cellar. They somehow knew that it would be the last night. The shelling had stopped. A sharp-edged moon observed them in the darkness of their room until Lejla lowered the blind, watching the plastic fall past the reflection of her own stricken eyes.

She had not been able to tell Marko about the baby after she slid into bed beside him, nor any of the times that night when he had awakened only to find her feigning sleep, her face wet with tears that she let slip onto her pillow. Nor even the next morning, when she had come so suddenly awake.

Then there had been no time for her to tell him before being "evacuated" from the house. She packed only one bag for them both, mechanically filling it with clothing and food. Opening her jewelry box, she wrapped necklaces and rings in a cloth, placing the bundle at the bottom of the bag beneath some heels of bread. The deutsche marks that she kept in a tin over the refrigerator went into the waistband of her stockings. Before they left the house, she handed Marko his woolen hat. He took it and the bag without saying anything.

And there was little time to talk when they were ordered out onto the road, Marko walking beside her, linking his arm in hers. She had come close, though, before he unwittingly deflected her confession.

"You were right, *mila*. It wasn't the right time." His voice was flat and she became uncertain.

Trucks speeding past them spat gravel from beneath thick tires and they could see people standing in the beds, crammed against the sideboards. Each time a truck passed, Lejla scanned the faces for someone she knew, for her parents or for Marko's.

Several times she thought she heard a timid voice call out to her: *Lejla!* But each time she looked up, she was unable to find its source. Marko, walking silently beside her, seemed not to have noticed.

Nearing the middle of town, they could see people converging on the old mosque. It had been converted into a "collection center," the sterile phrase which men had been repeating through megaphones all along the road to town.

In the courtyard stood an old stone fountain where the faithful washed their feet. Years ago, an art historian had come from Sarajevo to take pictures of it. His article later appeared in a Western journal with glossy color photographs of the mosque's courtyard. There was one of the fountain, green climbing vines wreathing a stone canopy, which Lejla had clipped and kept in a notebook at home.

Now she climbed the steps in her shoes, her face rigid as she stepped over the threshold. She had not been in the mosque since childhood. But, in stepping onto the richly colored rugs, she swayed suddenly, stabbed through by a memory of her grandmother, who had prayed five times a day until her death. Even when arthritis had buckled her legs and she was unable to pray comfortably on the floor, she would place her prayer rug on the kitchen table and, seated, bend to rest her forehead against it. Playing under the table, Lejla would grow quiet for this ceremony.

I prayed with you then, she remembered. Crouched at her grandmother's feet, eyelids shut tight, she would flutter her lips in imitation of the old woman. She had not known the words to the prayers, had not even known that the faint whispers from above represented language in any regular sense. But she had been earnest in her emulation, returning to her conversations with dolls only once she heard the chair being pushed back from the table.

Inside the mosque, she and Marko were ushered to a table where a humorless woman sat, a thick stack of computer printouts before her. She found their names on the list and slid a piece of paper across the table to them.

"Sign here." She indicated a line on the paper. "And then you'll be processed and sent to Germany on the next convoy."

Lejla lowered her head and read aloud. "We the undersigned surrender all our property . . ."

She trailed off, looking at Marko as the woman tapped her pen against the table impatiently. The document was illegal, Lejla knew. But the city would be under occupation now, anyway. If it was ever freed, the paper would mean nothing. If it was not, they would be unable to live there.

Lejla signed after Marko. She made the *L* big, so that her sloping script joined her name to the blocky letters of his.

They began pushing men to one side of the mosque and women to the other.

She clung to Marko's hand until the last possible minute. "Marko . . ."

"It will be all right," he told her, but she could see that he was far from sure.

A woman started to cry behind them.

He touched the dark braid that hung across her shoulder. She wore her hair in one plait when she was at home, cooking or reading the newspaper with him on their bed. He liked to hold the braid in his hand, unraveling it as he kissed her.

"*Zamirisa kosa, ko zumbuli plavi,*" he sang under his breath in the middle of the crowded mosque. "*The smell of her hair, like blue hyacinth.*"

A roar like a forest fire rose through her chest. "There's something . . ." she started wildly.

But a new group of men, dressed in camouflage, had entered the mosque. They flowed through the bewildered people like a river, running between them and around them and stranding them like human islands. She herself was carried away, twisting to look over her shoulder to where Marko had been standing. But a soldier directly behind her pushed her so that she almost fell, and Marko was gone.

She could hear snatches from the low conversations of the newly arrived men. Some of the men in camouflage she recognized from town. Others were old classmates from high school. She saw her math teacher, and when they made eye contact, she thought that he was about to call out to her. Instead he turned his back and started talking quietly with the men next to him. A moment later they burst into laughter.

There were men who owned businesses in town and even neighbors. But they looked through her as if she had been away for years and had returned with another's face.

"This is the way you usually do it," she heard one slurred voice say as the separation continued. And as she joined the group of women, she realized that some of the uniformed men were drunk. She could smell the *rakija*, the odor so sweet and sickening that it yellowed the air in front of her.

Lejla looked at the swirling room around her, detached enough to feel as if she stood in the eye of the storm. She tried to find the familiar shape of Marko's lowered head, the shirt he was wearing which she had ironed only days before. But she was surrounded by a crowd of bewildered faces, a kaleidoscope of gray skin and unhappy eyes.

"Lejla!" A voice called out to her, and she turned to see Marko's sister, Mira, pushing through the crowd.

"Where's Marko?" her sister-in-law asked. Lejla noticed that the woman's wide black pupils were static. She wondered if her own eyes had that center of frightened black.

"He's over there with the other men. Where's your father? Have you seen mine?"

Mira shook her head. "I don't know. We were separated before we ever got into the trucks." Her eyes filled with tears, and she was carried in one direction by the shoving of the crowd, pressed hard against the wall.

Lejla was about to grab her sleeve to prevent their separation when another commotion started beside her. An older woman had a desperate hold on her son's hand. "He's only a child!" she wailed. "He should stay with me!"

The uniformed men closed in around her, dragging the startled-looking youth away into the crowd. The woman's sobs hovered over the heads in the mosque.

"For the love of God," another woman pleaded. "Be quiet. You're going to make it worse for him. For all of us."

A man had climbed onto a chair near the doorway, and began to speak through a megaphone. "Listen to me. You will all be reunited once we take down some information. We are only separating you because we hope to exchange some of your men for our prisoners . . ."

The people in the mosque looked at one another.

The man with the megaphone went on, "We need to draw up lists of men for the exchange, and women will be sent in trucks directly to your people on the other side of the lines. We will not harm any of you, but you must cooperate."

And then, suddenly, they were being herded toward the mosque doors.

"Lejla!" It was her sister, Emina, pushing her way through the surging crowd. Their mother was behind her, hanging on to the belt loop of Emina's jeans.

Lejla began to cry, and the three of them held on to each other, all the while being pushed outside, toward several trucks that were lined up on the street.

When it was their turn to clamber into one of the trucks, they pushed their mother up from behind. Lejla was about to give her sister a hand up when a man stepped out of the line of soldiers overseeing the loading.

"Not you two," he said curtly.

Their mother began to shriek, but another man stepped out to lift the gate of the truck. He struck the metal with the flat of his hand, making a hollow sound that seemed to vibrate in Lejla's rib cage like the ringing of a deep bell. The truck lurched forward, and Lejla could see her mother's frantic face over the side.

"Lejla! Emina!" she was shrieking.

The two younger women were dragged to another truck and pushed up roughly. Together they landed in the truck bed, where other women helped them sit up. When the truck was full, a tarp was lowered and they were sealed in complete darkness, filled with the sound of weeping. But even then Lejla could hear the timid inflections above the sobs of the other women. She covered her belly with her hands, listening to the little voice.

Will you tell our children how their father had to walk eight kilometers to see their mother every night? Marko had asked when they both finished university and began courting.

Lejla's father would not allow her to go into town to meet

him. *If he wants to see you, he can walk out here.* And, doubting his intentions, had likewise doubted that his visits would occur with any regularity.

Young people are lazy, she overheard him telling her mother. *He'll tire soon enough.*

Lejla had protested. *He doesn't have a car.*

All the better, her father had retorted.

But each evening Marko had appeared in their yard, asking Lejla if she would like to take a walk.

A walk, her father would snort from behind his newspaper. *Haven't you walked enough?*

Their wedding lasted until morning. It was summertime and people crowded the town hall, singing, drinking, and spilling out onto the street. Her father toasted the couple, his voice growing gruff as he recounted Marko's persistence. "I said to myself, This boy . . ." He lifted his glass with an impish expression. "This boy I want for a son."

And the wedding guests, many of whom had witnessed Marko trotting through snow, rain, and wind, dissolved into laughter.

Later, she watched Emina, who was then still in school, whirl past in a cloud with her sweetheart Suad. He was a tall, shy boy, but on that night his face was flushed and his eyes bright.

When they were all exhausted from dancing and a little drunk, one of Marko's cousins started teasing Lejla's younger sister, breaking into song about another Emina. The song, from a poem by Aleksa Šantić, tells the story of a man who passes a jasmine-filled garden where a young woman is filling a watering can. Awed by the girl's beauty and grace, he calls out to her. But she will have nothing to do with him and his love goes unrequited.

Emina had reddened at the words, and someone slapped Suad on the back. But a strange quiet soon descended on the crowd and Lejla became uneasy listening to the song . . . *Slalomljen je ibrik, uvelo je cvijeće* . . . *The watering can is broken, the garden overgrown* . . . *The old poet is dead.* Lejla's hand twitched violently, nearly overturning a wineglass. *And Emina has died.*

"This is a wedding, not a funeral!" someone shouted in protest, and the musicians roused themselves to start another song. People began to dance once again and Marko kissed away her frown, laughing as people started to whistle.

From the truck the women were led into a concrete building, down a corridor and into a windowless, unlit storage room. She and Emina sat on the cement floor, their backs against a wall.

Lejla leaned her head against the hard, rough surface, the conversations floating around her like birds in a children's cartoon. Every once in a while one would flutter near enough that a few words penetrated her fog.

"I didn't see him in the line . . ."

". . . they're dead . . ."

". . . cousins in Germany . . ."

She and Marko had been trying to have a baby for a year, ever since the war had started in neighboring Croatia. Marko's was one of the few Croatian families in the town, and his older brother had left to join the fight. Things would be harder on Marko, wherever they had taken him.

"It's not the right time," she had told him at first. "Who knows what is going to happen. It's wrong to bring a baby into this."

But she had not convinced him. "Lejla," he had told her, "it's never the right time. Let's just let nature take its course."

Not getting pregnant had both disappointed and relieved her. But on the day that the Crisis Committee formed, staffed exclusively by Serbs who had uniformed themselves overnight, she realized that she had not menstruated in six weeks.

She had not told Marko in those first weeks. She had wanted to be sure. There was almost no morning sickness, and she did not want to raise his hopes. Later, she had not wanted to burden him more than he already was.

He doesn't even know, a voice wailed inside her head, but she quieted it immediately. She would tell him when they were reunited in Croatia or Germany, or wherever they were going. They had all been promised safe passage out of Bosnia.

That night they took three teenage girls out of the room. The girls, whose names had been called from a piece of paper, had risen uncertainly to their feet. Lejla recognized two of them as the imam's daughters. She could hear music and men's laughter from the other side of the door.

A stunned silence descended on the women when the door slammed shut and darkness again covered them.

"Maybe they're going to be freed in an exchange," one voice whispered tremulously, breaking the silence.

Someone from the other end of the room snorted loudly. "Don't be stupid."

When the door opened hours later, two of the girls were thrown back into the room. The music reached a dizzying pitch, making the air in front of Lejla's eyes vibrate as she blinked from the sudden light.

The sound of the two girls crying had gone on for a long time.

Lejla pulled her knees to her chest and leaned her forehead against them. When she felt Emina shivering beside her, she straightened, putting an arm around her sister's shoulders.

Emina curled up into a ball and lay her head in Lejla's lap. Her mouth was moving soundlessly in the dark and Lejla dropped a hand to stroke her hair. Emina's trembling jaw made a rhythm against her leg and Lejla concentrated, trying to discover if the soundless words were a prayer or a song.

There are deaths that happen only in the dark, she thought her sister was saying.

When the door was again unlocked, hours later, there was a scrambling as women tried to back away. A man entered the room carrying a powerful flashlight. Its beam cut across downcast and terrified faces, all looking down.

And in the middle of it all, the baby was singing to Lejla. She looked at her sister. "Do you hear that, Emina?" she whispered.

"Shhhh. Be quiet." Emina sat up stiffly and reached around Lejla's neck to cover her mouth.

But Lejla could hear the little voice. It was strong for all its small size, and reminded her of an aria. Something about an alignment of sun and stars, and the sound the sea makes when you are underwater.

"I think this is the one." She felt one of the men stand in front of her, ordering her to rise.

There's something I need to tell you, Emina, she thought, getting to her feet unsteadily.

Her sister's small face was white in the flashlight's beam, the skin under her eyes blue with tears.

"*Budi jaka*. Be strong," she told Emina, and then leaned in, whispering the words so quietly she wondered if she had said them aloud or just thought them.

But her sister nodded swiftly and placed a hand across her own belly to show that she understood.

Now you exist, Lejla thought.

She was led down a long hall, out of the building, and across a courtyard to another smaller structure. It appeared to be an old factory complex, although she recognized none of the buildings. She had tried to map out the truck's turns in her head, but they had been too numerous and the journey had been too long.

She was pushed into a room with a dirty uncovered mattress. The door swung shut and she listened to the footsteps receding. They grew fainter in the distance and she imagined her sister being led out of the room. *Now you are real.* Later, she remembered the yawning silence on the other side of her door.

The little voice talked to her, despite the days during her imprisonment when she would not respond, angry, thinking she was losing her mind.

Time seemed to slow down in the small room, the air converting itself into a thick and sluggish substance. Later, she could not remember whether hours or days had elapsed before she heard footsteps in the hall outside. A man who had been a friend in that other life let himself into the room quietly, and she raised her tearstained face. But her relief lasted only a moment, shriveling when she took in his expressionless features.

He sat down on the mattress beside her and lit a cigarette, offering her one from the pack, but she shook her head.

"Have you become so virtuous, Lejla?" he asked with a little smile. "You used to smoke."

She was silent, watching him. He had been friends with Marko in high school. They had grown up in the same neighborhood, playing soccer in the street.

"You were at our wedding," she told him.

He did not seem to hear her.

"You were at our wedding," she repeated, almost angrily.

His eyes flashed. "Not much is the same since then."

She swallowed with great difficulty. "Marko was your friend."

He shrugged. "Marko is an Ustaša. He stopped being my friend when his brother went to fight with the fascists."

"We were your friends," she told him again.

His voice was without inflection, so flat that it made her wince. He threw his cigarette on the floor. "Those friendships are dead."

The voice was crying. It was howling like a little wolf.

Lejla was hovering on the edge of consciousness, skirting it like a dancer onstage, clinging to the periphery of darkness.

You're ruined, she told the voice.

It stopped crying immediately.

They've polluted you.

There was a commotion in the hall outside her room. Her

eyes flickered open and the baby seemed to retreat. She closed them, hearing shouting and laughter. Unsure whether she was dreaming, she felt some shade of herself rise to its feet and lean against the door.

"Lejla!" It was her sister's voice and Lejla began to pound the door with her fists. She beat it as she had seen a boxer in a film punch a suspended bag, hands moving in rapid-fire succession. She bloodied her hands on the doors, the baby screaming in horror.

They had the power to infiltrate her dreams, their faces a continuing presence even when she slipped from consciousness. In the dreams she tore barefoot from one nightmare to the next, as if they were horror-filled towns and the roads between them a grim respite where she hung in painful suspension, just beneath the surface of waking.

It was a torturous conversion, in which the world lost its soft color and bland edges. In the dreams, she cut herself on air, spraying blood in wide arcs, leaving stains as thick and greasy as gasoline.

She died repeatedly in her dreams, throwing herself from the mosque's tall minaret and splintering on the white stone of the courtyard below, or grabbing her captor's gun and firing it again and again through her forehead. She could chart the burning path of the bullets, squeezing her eyes tightly in expectation, but was unable to die successfully.

After these failed somnambulic attempts, she took in her surroundings from the grave of her body. It seemed that a wasteland stretched infinitely in all directions. But each time the key turned noisily in the lock, she was violently resurrected.

Not even in my dreams, she whimpered into her hands.

And then one night, toward the end of her captivity, Marko sat on the edge of their bed at home, his naked back to her. And when she leaned toward him, knowing full well that it was a dream, she expected a trick. That was the way in which they operated, after all. She expected him to crumble into dust beneath her hands or turn around bearing a stranger's face.

But as she leaned to bury her face in the back of his neck, the dream bore his scent.

When she was finally released, she was made to walk over kilometers of roads and fields that had been mined. She walked with a purpose that few of the other women straggling toward free territory shared. It was on that walk that she began to listen again. The voice echoed throughout the no-man's-land, where the barest crescent of a moon guided her steps.

How could it be that they did not kill you? How could it be that you survived?

And the voice continued, like a cricket chirruping into the night. Sometimes singing, sometimes sighing. At times it even laughed, and she smiled to hear it laughing.

When she reached the refugee center in Zagreb, the other women looked at her strangely. They nudged each other meaningfully. And it was there that her mother found her, huddled in one corner of a room.

The older woman crouched beside her, taking the strange, thin face in her hands. "Lejla?" she whispered.

There was no recognition in her daughter's face. "What are

you saying?" Lejla was asking, placing a hand on her stomach. "What do you want to tell your mama?"

"Lejla," her own mother said more insistently.

There was a giggle from the other end and she smiled knowingly. "Yes, yes. You're right. It's over now."

In Zagreb, a doctor at the refugee center examined her. They estimated that she was five months pregnant.

The doctor hesitated a moment and said, "The baby seems healthy."

She nodded and looked at him expectantly.

"We have a lot of women like yourself coming in here."

She waited.

"You were in a camp?"

She shrugged, feeling her ears start to burn. *I wish I were a man*, she told the doctor in her head. *I wish I were a man who could take a gun and go off to war. I wish I could find him and kill him.*

The doctor lowered his face and began examining his pencil. "There are options. The pregnancy is too progressed to terminate, but . . ."

She lowered her gaze to the hands in her lap. "The baby is my husband's."

He looked at her dubiously.

"I was pregnant when we were separated."

He seemed relieved by this and nodded. "Good, good." The faint hiss as he let all the air out of his lungs had not escaped her. "Do you have any news about your husband?"

"No." She shook her head. "I'm waiting for him. They say he's dead. I want to wait for him, and then we'll go on to Germany together."

He seemed to falter. She rose and picked up her bag.

He continued to follow her in nightmares. She could hear his derisive laughter as he said her name. *Lejla.* Like something ugly. All her daytime bravado fled her in those dreams, all elaborate fantasies about his death foundering, and she would waken in a panic, the first few moments of consciousness always a shock.

In the next camp, on the outskirts of Munich, she and her mother shared a room with four other Bosnian women. They allowed each day to burn down to its conclusion, like a forgotten cigarette, waiting for Emina and their husbands.

"When did you last see her?" Her mother had insisted on hearing everything.

And Lejla had told her about the truck and the room crammed with women. She told her about their separation.

Her mother watched her with large eyes. "I knew, I knew . . ." She rocked back and forth.

"The baby is Marko's," Lejla told her.

The older woman stilled and buried her face in her hands.

They heard that the mosque had been destroyed, and that in its place was a parking lot. She no longer had the clipping of the mosque's stone fountain and spent days sifting through old journals in a Munich archive until she found the article again. Her heart had skipped to see the photographs—the fountain's carving and the curling green vines now existed solely in pictures, and the images made her eyes burn. When the respectable Frau who manned the reading room turned her back, she ripped the pages furtively from the magazine, folding them and placing them in her bag. On the return bus ride to the refugee center, she hung on to a plastic overhead strap and watched the slate-colored sky go by. *This is how we regain the past,* she told her rain-spattered reflection. *Centimeters at a time.* Lejla pictured her sister's shadow wandering through their town's broken lines, stubborn and ghostly, the guardian of memory.

When Marko was released from a camp, together with her father, they were reunited in a government-subsidized apartment in Germany. They made plans to emigrate to Canada. She did not tell him what had happened, but it was months before he could hold her in the same way, and she was sure that he had guessed. She had also seen the way he stood by the baby's crib, never certain whether he looked upon some trace of self, or the face of someone he should hate.

"She's yours," Lejla had told him.

He had nodded, but was unable to meet her eyes.

"Give him time," her mother had said.

And each night when they entered sleep, they entered it separately. And when she awoke from her battles, the bullet-riddled Lejla who threw herself from great heights turning into the conscious Lejla, she could see in Marko's eyes that he had also made his way back from some vile ground. And they held hands wordlessly in the bed, lost in their own impenetrable thoughts, shaking off the pollution of their dreams.

This is how we reach each other, Lejla would tell the ceiling above their bed. *Through kilometers of tainted air.*

In some of the dreams, Emina follows her through the mined

fields. Their heels burn over the kilometers they walk, beating a steady path toward free territory. Fires start in the fields on either side, and they hurry down the smoky tunnel between. She can hear the whispering behind her, and stops to let her sister catch up. But when she turns around, the fires have ceased and there is nothing behind her except for a cold moon. The voice continues, rising on smoke out of the dusty ground. *Pjesma o Emini, nikad umrijet' neće*, it tells her. *Emina's song will never die.*

Surveillance

ON A DAY IN EARLY SPRING, a nondescript man stood under bare trees and a sky white with unshed snow. Through the lens of a camera he was observing a woman washing windows in a building across the street. He was able to confine her within the camera's crosshairs so that even with the sweeping movements of her arms she was boxed between the thin black lines. Beneath his lens, she looked like a small metallic fly moving delicate legs and wings. It struck him that he knew her best, and only, through glass.

He had watched her at this chore before. First she washed the glass from the inside, a gray rag sliding under her hand in circles. It obliterated her face, then her neck and chest. Waiting for her to open the window and clean the exterior pane of glass, he realized that he had been holding his breath and exhaled sharply. At this unseen cue, she opened the window and leaned out into the air. A gust of wind caught her brown hair, as if she had suddenly escaped the pull of gravity, and he imagined that it was a part of him, until recently kept buried in his lungs, that had touched her face.

Today she was wearing faded jeans and a T-shirt. When she climbed barefoot onto the sill in order to reach the left window, which was jammed, he felt a sliding in his chest, as if two surfaces along a fault line had suddenly released their grip.

"Careful, Lena," he said softly. He did not remember when he had begun to address her directly.

But she cleaned the glass unworriedly, balancing two stories above the concrete sidewalk, and never once looked down. When finished, she turned neatly to climb back into the apartment. It was at the midpoint of her pivot that he took the shot, freezing her in profile.

The Bureau liked random shots of people engaged in their everyday lives. It helped throw detainees off-balance during interrogations.

How long have you been watching me? they would ask in shock.

How long do you think? they would respond, bringing out still more photographs of mundane tasks. It was only later that they would bring out the incriminating pictures—pictures that made the temperature rise suddenly in airless rooms.

He wasn't cut out for conducting interrogations. He was a photographer.

The park in which he was standing was wet and cold but offered a sheltered vantage from which to survey her building. He shivered in his jacket, continuing to watch her through the lens. She moved behind the blind of a thick wall, emerging finally in another window which she began to wash as well. He was too far away to see the texture of her skin, but he imagined the gooseflesh that must have been covering her bare arms and neck after the cold-air balancing act.

When footsteps echoed behind him, he sensed rather than saw the approach of an old man and his dog. He lowered the camera, listening to the man's scolding tone.

"Outside, Bernard. You must do it outside." The old man did not even glance in his direction.

He raised the camera again to his face and focused, compressing the space around her. She was just closing the second window, pushing the glass shut from the inside. It seemed to him that she hesitated as she did this, hands holding the window latch at an awkward angle, face pressed to the outside. Her eyes were wide and dark and he turned abruptly and hurried back to the van. As he walked, he imagined that the gauze of the curtains, rolled and tucked to one side, floated back to the window and swung gently from side to side like a pendulum before becoming completely still.

His was a face that few people remembered and he was pleased at his ability to disappear in crowds. When he was younger, this anonymity had dismayed him. His teachers could never remember his name and women often overlooked him in favor of louder, more aggressive men.

When asked to describe him, no one could ever remember whether his eyes were closely set, how tall he was, or even the color of his hair. His face was so bland that he was able to observe people for years without their knowing. He followed them on city buses, waited behind them to buy roasted chestnuts in winter, and even assisted them from time to time with directions. And each time they looked through him, as if he himself were made of glass.

He had testified in one case against a university professor, following two years of surveillance.

"But I don't know you!" the man on the stand had nearly wailed, removing his spectacles to wipe them, replacing them a moment later. "I've never seen you before in my life."

Faceless, he had smiled.

They had been watching Lena for a month. The sound technician, a barrel-chested man with whom he had not previously worked, had introduced himself simply as Bear. Bear recorded her telephone conversations, leaving him to photograph her comings and goings. In her file at the Bureau, there were many Lenas. She appeared in a slew of black-and-white pictures, bundled in a woolen coat, talking to the downstairs neighbor, inspecting potatoes and carrots at the vegetable market. On warmer days, she stretched beside the window, the sill like a barre, and he had frozen her in her contortions. When the damp wind sank its teeth until it pierced his bones, she stood at the shut window in a thick sweater sipping coffee from a shallow cup that she held in both hands. In the pictures she was usually looking out. He liked to think that she had caught sight of something she had been expecting.

He knew the exact geography of her rooms because, one day, he had entered her apartment when she was at the theater for a dress rehearsal. They were to perform *La Bayadère*. When the show opened, he read the review of the opening night and added it to her file.

He had volunteered for the job of planting listening devices. Bear, who preferred to sit in the van looking at pornographic magazines of women with improbable anatomies, had merely shrugged.

The flimsy lock was no match for him and he let himself in quickly, standing for a moment in the quiet entrance hall and listening to the hissing of her radiators. The listening devices fit into the wooden grooves underneath the coffee table and on the back of the bathroom mirror. In the bedroom he had hesitated, fingering a corner of her thick comforter and opening her closet. Her scent glided out of the latter as if on feet, and he spent a moment looking at neatly folded sweaters and leather shoes. This intimacy satisfied him, and in the end he had left the bedroom unbugged.

Her lover's name was Andrei and he had left her the night before she washed the windows. They had arrived home together from her performance and run almost drunkenly up the stairs to the front door. The photographer had watched the man bury his nose in her hair as she fumbled for the key in her purse. *Lena*, he had imagined the man whispering, and found himself shivering in the dark.

"Lena," he said aloud in the deserted park, startling himself with the sound of his voice.

It seemed to him that she looked up suddenly, as if she had heard him. But the door had opened and swung shut and he had seen the light in the hall. Moments later, a light came on in her apartment. He waited until it was extinguished and watched the dark windows, shifting from foot to foot, imagining undressing her. He emptied his lungs, the fogged breath dancing in front of his face. He imagined laying her down on the large bed with its heavy walnut headboard. Her soft exhalations would run in shivers across his skin, and he imagined her eyes, half shut.

Later, she stood naked at the window, the light of the street-lamp icy on her breasts. He watched her until he saw a pair of arms creep around her from behind and turn her softly so that the moon glanced off the smooth white of her back.

When he slid back into the van, Bear was wearing the earphones and looked at him with a smile. He flashed a thumbs-up sign, mouthing, *They're fucking*, and offered to let him hear.

He declined.

A moment later Bear took off the headset a little disgustedly. "Why didn't you bug the bedroom?"

His only response was to shrug and open a magazine which he pretended to read. But he could not concentrate and the words on the page seemed to disengage from the paper.

Bear had replaced the headphones, sighing at intervals. Setting down the magazine, the photographer studied Bear and imagined with some revulsion that the large man beside him in the van was becoming excited. The technician was smiling, listening raptly. When it was over the man threw down the headset again and sighed. "You should have bugged the bedroom."

The whispered words the next morning were at frequencies too low even for the heavy equipment in the van to pick up, and sur-faced on tape only as strange sighs and hums. A short time later,

Andrei descended the steps rapidly, his face a tight and controlled mask. Lena watched him from the window.

Usually Andrei stopped in the street and waved up at her. He would blow a kiss to the naked woman at the window and she would pretend to catch it in the palm of her hand, eating it like a piece of fruit.

But that morning he did not stop and turn. He did not look over his shoulder and the photographer standing behind the tree in the park opposite knew that their strange dance had reached its conclusion.

Looking at the woman in the window, he felt that she knew it, too.

Coincidentally, he was familiar with Andrei's work. He was able to identify the distinctive colors and brushstrokes before the paintings were banned. He knew the name of the small country town in which Andrei had been born. They had been together at the Art Academy and knew each other by sight, never enough to do more than nod at one another, exchanging words only occasionally. He had been all but invisible then as well.

The Bureau had broken into Andrei's studio more than once, slashing canvases and snapping paintbrushes. They had left bottles of paint overturned in concentric circles of color that bled together, causing a kaleidoscope on the studio floor. To his relief, he had not been included in these missions.

He imagined the way Andrei must have told Lena that he was leaving, thought he could even pinpoint the afternoon on the basis of her tears, which he observed from a short distance away. The couple had been too careful to use the telephone or talk aloud in the apartment. The headphones had relayed a rustling of paper, and when they left the building, he had followed them at a distance. They stopped on a city bridge and he had stood on the stone promenade along the shoreline.

She was watching Andrei with a puzzled expression and he realized that she still did not know. Andrei drew her into an embrace but her back went rigid in her coat and she stared at him. She burst into tears and he saw the man's mouth moving against her ear. *Lena, Lena, Lena.*

Come with me, he would be asking her.

No, she was replying, shaking her head. *No.*

And, standing on the promenade, pretending to be taking pictures of ducks, he had been relieved.

Andrei escaped the country successfully. The train ticket they found in his bedroom bureau went unused and he had not returned home. They surmised later that he had started out on foot, dressed in the clothes from his last night with Lena. He had left wearing her smell.

Two days later the phone let out a sharp scream in her apartment.

He picked up the extra set of headphones and listened.

"Hello?" she was asking.

There was silence from the other side.

"Hello?" she asked again.

And again silence. Bear turned up the volume until they could hear a man breathing. The soft exhalations existed at a level beneath sound.

The caller broke the connection from his side. She stayed several moments longer on the phone before replacing it in its cradle.

This ceremony repeated itself in the days that followed, always between three and four in the afternoon.

In the evenings he took the streetcar home, walking the last few blocks to his empty flat. His building was one in a series of a thousand identical ones. He had once become lost in his own neighborhood after drinking nearly an entire bottle of brandy. His eyes had been unable to focus on numbers and he had wandered the gray complexes until dawn.

The apartment now housed his own collection of her pictures. The Bureau carefully recorded every roll of film allotted him, but in the safety of the darkroom he often developed more than one print. He had pictures of her dancing by her windows and leaning over the sill with a smile, talking to the neighbor's son who played soccer in the street. He had pictures of her with Andrei, walking hand in hand in front of the theater.

In the darkroom, he sat in the middle of the ghostly sheets of hanging wet paper, watching her face emerge from each of them. Lena sad. Lena happy. Lena after making love, when her lips were dark and her hair curled around her face.

Lena, he told the pictures, the breath from the song of her name making them sway on the line.

"Lena, it's your mother."

"Mama, I can't talk now." Her voice was sharp. It was 3:21.

"Lena, what is going on with you?" the woman wailed. "I haven't heard from you in days."

"Mama"—her voice was tense—"I'll call you later. Please, hang up the phone."

"Lena . . ."

"Now!" she shouted.

After three months, the calls became increasingly sporadic. He sensed her desperation in the few wordless interchanges. He could feel Andrei slipping away and knew that she felt it, too.

One day, she broke their rule and spoke. "I can't stand this silence." She began to cry. "I can't stand that you are farther and farther away. Each time, you are farther away."

And the quiet on the other side had been shocked, and Bear turned up the volume. They had caught the sudden intake of breath and the click when he hung up the phone, more abruptly this time than before.

There were no phone calls for two days.

For two days she did not go out and she did not come near the window. They could hear her moving from room to room, her footsteps hollow and lethargic. For two days she did not emerge from her apartment and an understudy filled in her performances.

On the third day, he climbed out of the van at 3:36. "I'm going for a walk," he told Bear.

He walked six blocks to a series of call boxes and dialed her number. His hand was shaking and he listened as it rang three times.

"Hello?" she asked, breathlessly.

He could feel her smile at the silence and smiled himself. He closed his eyes for a moment and let her listen to the sound of his breathing before breaking the connection.

When he clambered into the van, Bear did not even look up. "He called again."

His only response was to grunt.

He did this only once. There were no more phone calls.

Because he had access to foreign press at the Bureau, he knew that Andrei married an actress in Munich a year after his escape. A German magazine carried the story and he clipped it carefully, sending it to her in the mail and imagining how she would touch the same paper he had touched.

The next day, they listened to her humming as she entered the apartment. He heard her kick off her shoes and put water to boil for coffee. He even heard her mutter under her breath as, flipping through her mail, she came across the unfamiliar handwriting.

He imagined the puzzled look on her face. There was an interval and then she started to scream.

She sent the furniture in the apartment crashing, howling as she went. They heard glass breaking, a mirror or a vase. They listened to a violent shattering as its pieces sprayed the wooden floor. They could hear her crunching through them, like razor-sharp gravel, as she found other things to overturn.

A neighbor started beating on the wall, telling her to be quiet. Bear was looking with a puzzled expression at the audiotape moving from one spool to another. "What the hell is going on?"

His only response had been to shrug, listening to muffled crying as she flung herself onto the walnut bed.

They closed their investigation. *Citizen L appears to have no further contact with dissidents abroad*, he wrote in his notes. Her file was relegated to the Archive, among thousands of others. Then the Bureau was disbanded and he was in charge of burning his notes and the photographic archives of his cases. They all stood morosely over steel drums in the courtyard, feeding the glossy pages to the flames.

But when he got to her pictures, he could not destroy them. *The rest was not art*, he told himself. He opened a folder marked Lena 1. A smile spread slowly across his face as he imagined a photography exhibit that would bear her name. A retrospective of his work. *Portraits of Lena*.

He spared only that box, taking it back into the building when he had finished burning the others. The people inside the Bureau were in a panic and paid no attention to him. He walked coolly out the front door and into the street.

In his kitchen at home he rifled through the box. He pored over every shot, held each negative up to the light. When he finished, early the next morning, a smile touched his face. He thought, *How many nights we have spent together without your knowing.*

The envelopes were stacked, Lena 1 through Lena 12. They represented his life's work and he began to shake from the intimacy they contained.

The man has been watching her for some time on the tram. She turns her back on him, refolding the newspaper so that she can read it one-handed while holding on to the bar above her head. But she cannot concentrate on the article she is reading, something about corruption in the old government and dissidents abroad. Andrei's face emerges in her thoughts and she pushes it back angrily. But he returns, and for a moment she lets herself be touched by his hands.

She lets his mouth travel from one shoulder blade to the other, allows his forehead to press itself against her stomach. Last week she had been unable to conjure his face. The shape of his finger-nails and the lines on his hands had eluded her, but now here he is again, invisible and making love to her on a city tram.

A few stops later, she looks up. The strange man is still there, watching her with a small smile, and she wonders if she knows him. When the tram makes its next stop she darts out the doors at the last minute, hearing them shut with a grating sound behind her. It pulls away and she sees that she is alone on the street in a residential neighborhood. She avoids looking up at the windows as the tram passes, feeling his gaze on her lowered head. She senses even his vague puzzlement.

She pictures the imaginary Andrei leaning easily against the back windows as the stranger had done, suddenly nonplussed by her quick maneuver. She can imagine his hesitancy, and then a smile, at once sad and appreciative. *Well done, Lena*, she can imag-ine him teasing.

She looks around her in the gray evening and shifts the bag on her shoulder. It is filled with potatoes and carrots she had stopped to buy at the marketplace on the way home. She can still see the very back of the tram and watches its slow turn. The white face at the rear window is not Andrei's, but she throws it a quick, dismis-sive wave nonetheless, just before it disappears behind some buildings.

"He's gone," she tells the air, and sets off on foot in the oppo-site direction.

Suspension

"OLD MAN." Omer Hadžić says the words to himself quietly. He is looking into the cracked piece of glass he hung over the porcelain sink in the bathroom. He uses it for shaving, but lately he has been coming to stare at his reflection. Not registering much, just looking at the strange old face.

It is not like the first shock, two years before, when he had been freed from the camp in a prisoner exchange. The gauntness of the face in the shopwindow of an emptied store in Travnik had startled him. Initially he had not recognized it as his own. It was the threadbare shirt that he recognized, bewildered at first that another man should be wearing one so much like his own. It was a

workshirt that his wife had made, sitting quietly in their farm-
house, after the children were asleep and the dinner plates washed.

Now he explores the bones in his cheeks, the deep shadows
around his eyes. He is amazed by the gray hairs that have overtaken
most of the black hair. His skin is still as brown and supple as a
young man's. He curses himself silently. Such vanity was something he would expect of his daughter, something for which he
would shoo her away with a swat at her bottom, telling her to concentrate more on her chores than on her beauty.

He talks to the face. Quietly, so that his wife and daughter,
who are sleeping in the next room, do not hear. This time, a question rises in his mind, as inevitably as if it had been planted last sea-
son and spent all winter lying there, a tiny frozen embryo. Now,
after a good rain, it is lifting its green head out of the soil. He leans
on the sink, one hand placed on either side, and his face draws
closer to the old man's. Their noses are almost touching.

"Would my son have grown old like me, old man?"

If his wife had heard him, she would have corrected him
gently but firmly. Always drawing an extra chair to the table at
dinnertime, she insisted that the boy was alive. She marked his
birthday this year, cooking the *sarma* with cream as Edin liked it.
Omer is wordless in the face of her delusions. She talks of the boy
as if she has proof that he is alive in some camp or prison. It drives
him a bit mad. He raised his voice to her once. But catching sight
of the sad round eyes of his sixteen-year-old daughter, he rose from
the table so violently that the chair turned over, and fled outside.

He lights a cigarette from the candle he has carried into the
bathroom. The old man looks better through a curtain of smoke.
He flicks the ashes into the sink. *My son's face*, he thinks.

Omer is consumed by the memory of shoes.

Long before the war had started, Edin had saved money for a pair of white tennis shoes. They had high sides and laced up like boots. They were the ugliest things Omer had ever seen, and he told his son so. But Edin, who had bought them from a cousin who worked in Austria as a *Gastarbeiter*, was adamant. At fifteen, he would meet their neighbor's sons in the evening, and dressed in matching nylon tracksuits, they would set off down the road.

Once Omer had watched them depart, shaking his head in stupefaction. They reminded him of a group of shuffling yearlings. And even when it was evening and the sun had disappeared, he could see those white sneaker boots receding in the distance.

"How can you even lift your feet?" he had asked his son, joking. "No wonder you're so thin. You burn up twice as much energy as the average person, lifting those things."

Years later, the first thing he saw in the pile of garbage that greeted them in front of their half-destroyed home was one of those shoes. It wasn't even white anymore, more the tired color of old ash, and there were no laces.

When the newly appointed war government in town ordered all Moslems to hand in their weapons, heads of households in the village called an emergency meeting. Omer had gone there to meet his three brothers, leaving his wife and daughter at home. His son, nineteen, had accompanied him, and they were silent on the way to the designated house.

They talked until long past the curfew in the damp cellar of the house. There were few patrols in those days. The police rarely came through the village, tending instead to stick to the periphery, occasionally stopping people unlucky enough to be coming back from a market day or from visiting a friend in another village.

They had reached a deadlock. The older men opted for caution, the younger ones wanted action. Stories of shelled villages and slaughtered civilians had been filtering in from other regions. Time was running out.

"But we don't want conflict with them," his neighbor Nihad said. "If we do what they say, they'll leave us alone." Others nodded, but the younger men were increasingly restless.

"If we give them the weapons, we give them our only means of defense." Omer's nephew, Suad, spoke heatedly. He was older than the other youths, almost thirty, and had worked for some time in Switzerland. The younger ones were drawn to him.

"Where's your head?" Old Emir spat the words at him. "We're finished if we don't give them what they want." The week before, the Serbs had shelled a village farther upriver. He reminded them, "Do you recall what came floating down the river?" There was an uncomfortable silence. Two bloated bodies had washed ashore. They had been buried quietly and without ceremony.

"What do you want? Guerrilla warfare? Can you imagine what will happen to our wives and daughters if we hold out and are then defeated? And we will be defeated. We stand no chance against them." Omer's brother spoke bitterly.

"So we go like sheep to be butchered?"

Omer registered his son's words with surprise. He frowned slightly. Where had the boy gotten these ideas?

That night they cut through the fields back to their houses. His wife had been waiting for them. They removed their shoes, and she ushered them in. They sat on the couches and overstuffed cushions. Edin described the meeting to his mother. She looked from him to Omer, who held his hands palms up and shrugged.

That night he awoke to find her crying. She made no sound, but the shaking of her shoulders had roused him. He folded her into his arms. He knew she was asleep when the soft exhalations against his chest became even and deep. But he held her longer, looking at the pattern that the moonlight made on the ceiling of their room.

Four men had gathered the weapons and taken them into the town, where Serb officials assured them that they had saved their village from an uncertain fate. They returned weary but relieved.

The shelling began almost immediately. Omer ordered his family down to the basement. His wife had been prepared. She had already carried down cushions and candles. There were even tins of food. They spent three days in the cellar while the village was continuously shelled.

Finally, they heard a man yelling through a loudspeaker that they should all come out, that it was safe now, and if they hid they would be shot. They climbed the stairs mutely, into the sharp and pounding sunshine. They were told to walk in the direction of the mosque and joined people walking from other houses.

They were ordered into a school. Men were immediately separated from women, and he called out his wife's name as she and their daughter were taken away, but a soldier hit him with the butt of his rifle. He sank to his knees, refusing to avert his eyes from his wife's frantic expression and his daughter's tearstained face.

For two days men were continuously removed for questioning, and returned bloody and half-conscious. On the second night, Omer was called. Edin, who was sitting on the floor next to him, grabbed his arm so tightly that it hurt. Omer heard a whimper. It came from his own throat. He was afraid of what the guards would do if they had to come get him. So he shook the hand off. He was led into another, smaller room. The interrogators waiting inside were almost as young as his son, but he recognized none of them.

"Who are the Moslem extremists in your village? Who are the members of the SDA?" they began asking.

One pinned his arms behind his back as another punched him in the ribs. He doubled over, gasping, shaking his head. "I don't know," he pleaded with them, "I'm not a political man!"

The questioning went on for over an hour. Where were the guns hidden in the village? Had they given shelter or food to the Green Berets?

He was dragged back to the room, unable to walk alone. He collapsed on the floor. After a moment he opened his eyes. "Edin?"

Silence.

Panic gripped him, sucking all the air from his lungs. "Edin?" His voice was a whisper.

"They took all the young ones while you were gone, Omer." It was his brother's voice, dead and without inflection. "They took them."

He was released the next day for medical reasons. The guards had told him this with a smirk. He walked the five kilometers back to his home. He had bruises everywhere, even on the soles of his feet, which he had never known could bruise. His face was frozen, the dried blood making expression impossible. His wife came out into the yard crying, her mouth moving frantically, but he could not hear any sound.

"Izeta?" he managed to choke out. He saw his daughter's face in the kitchen window and registered her panicked expression and the way her eyes searched behind him for the ambling figure of her brother.

"Where is my Edin?" His wife's voice finally came through his consciousness. It sliced through the dumb silence like a knife. "Where is my boy?"

Three weeks later, his family was separated again. He was taken to a camp where he spent ten months. They were told that their wives and children would be transported across lines to safety, that the Army of Serbian Krajina did not hurt women or children.

In the camp, he lost all sense of time. He could barely register the change of the seasons. He was in a stupor until the day he saw his nephew's scarred face.

"Uncle"—the boy was weeping—"they have killed all my brothers."

Omer put his arm around the boy's shoulder. He had been separated out early on and taken for a work detail. He knew nothing about Edin, though he thought Omer's son had been sent to dig trenches.

Later, two other men from their village were transferred to the camp. One said he heard that Edin had been transferred to a jail in Banja Luka, but the other shook his head. No, he had been forced to cut wood for the army.

————

When he was released, an older woman and young girl were waiting for him in Travnik. He had to be helped down from the convoy truck by two younger men. The young girl embraced him and then peered into his face worriedly.

"Father," she was saying to him in a choked voice. "Father, it's me."

Last year, their town was liberated. The three of them returned to their house a week later. They are luckier than most, because although the entire structure will have to be torn down and rebuilt, there are two rooms on the first floor that suffice as temporary shelter. His daughter swears to him that with the thick plastic affixed to the windows, she can barely feel the wind at night.

They spent the end of the summer chopping firewood for the stove, which miraculously is still in its old place in the kitchen, even though not a stick of furniture can be found in the entire house. They have sifted through the ankle-deep detritus of the first floor, broken dishes, old papers, bullet casings. His wife attacked these rooms with a fury, determined to wipe out every fingerprint of those who had been there in the interim.

She carried water in a pail from the river. Even the dank smell of the lichened water is preferable to the smell of those swine in her house. She scrubs the floor until her knuckles are raw. It is the loss of the carpets and their soft cleanness that she minds the most. One had been a gift from her parents for their wedding. Now they must start anew.

Omer walks to the town where the Red Cross has set up an office. The woman there takes down the data. Edin Hadžić, who would now be twenty-three. Light brown hair, blue eyes. He was wearing jeans, a T-shirt, and a sweater that his mother had knitted for him. And work boots.

"Teeth?"

Omer doesn't understand the question at first. She explains to him that sometimes the only way to identify them, the anonymous bodies, is through defining characteristics of the teeth and bones.

He shakes his head. "His teeth were normal." He looks at his work-roughened hands and then remembers something. "Bones. You mean if he ever broke a bone?"

"Yes." She nods, waiting for him to continue.

He closes his eyes, remembering. Edin was twelve years old. They were helping build a neighbor's barn. They had all stopped to eat lunch under the coolness of a stand of trees. Edin and his friends were hiding behind the barn and smoking. The boys thought they had outwitted the adults, but the men sitting underneath the tree could smell it. Omer had opened a lazy eye and looked at his brother.

"They think we don't know," his brother had said, amused. "They don't know that was our spot as well."

Omer leaned his head back against the tree, closing his eyes again.

Seconds later his brother was yelling, "Get down from there!"

His eyes flashed open and he looked up to see his son balancing on one of the crossbeams of the barn. He jumped to his feet as he watched his son lean precariously and fall.

Now, in the whitewashed office, he remembers driving into

town, the boy silent in the seat beside him, wincing at every bump they hit. He is remembering his son, buoyed in the blue sky. A bird that suddenly wavered in flight.

"His arm," he says simply. "He broke his arm."

Some weeks later he hears from a neighbor who heard from a bus driver that there was an Edin Hadžić in jail in Prijedor. A week after that he hears that it wasn't Prijedor at all, but Sanski Most. Five days later he hears that his son is living as a refugee in Germany. It is the last option that his wife hopes for, mourning that the telephone lines are not repaired.

"How will our boy get in touch with us?" she asked her husband, worriedly at first. Then, more peacefully, "He'll know to look for us here. In his home."

But months pass. Omer is not sure. He has written letters to every agency he can find. But he has the feeling that each time he walks into town to deliver them, or to mail them, they are disappearing into space. A white, foggy space that robs the world of all sound, all feeling. This is where he believes his son exists.

Canis lupus

IN THE CONFINED SPACE of my cell I am a constant gray motion. I keep my head down as I pace and my breath rises in anxious clouds. The winter darkness is thick and the lamps which once showed the gleam of metal bars are long burned out. But my ashen complexion is perceptible as a faintly moving light. Back and forth, then back again.

The bars are darkness of a different consistency, an impenetrable grid against the sky. Periodically I slow behind them for faint catches in time, the interval it takes my heart to beat once. I come close to shoving my head between them before shying.

Never wholly stopping, I hover, and then continue my looping vigil. The low sounds in my throat are strange even to my own ears, and my legs ache at the knowledge of my captivity, as if driven through with metal teeth.

Filthy darkness, comes a voice from a short distance away. Another prisoner, I believe, and make myself silent in my pacing. Yet I am calmed by this strange communion. City darkness is filthy darkness, I agree. This is knowledge any country boy shares, and I wonder for a moment from which unsoiled territory he was seized, whether forest or sloping rock. The city's low canopy is stifling in all its variations, but the darkness for which I long is crisply pure, with edges of pine sharp against the sky. No smell of diesel or cement, none of the associated sounds of metal, the dull surfaces of plastic, or the razor edges of shattered glass.

In that immaculate and remembered darkness, sound traverses vast expanses in the space of seconds. I can chart the fall of rock, the movement of water in the distance. The instant a man steps through the trees, crunching snow underfoot, I feel his presence. Once I sensed these things below the surface of sound. But my instincts now are ruined, the qualities that made me an astute tracker lost and degraded.

There is a round of distant gunfire and a shell explodes in the yard outside, sending an arc of light through the bars. I halt, finally, feeling the angles of my face illuminated. The muscles in my shoulders convulse, and afterward, my blinded eyes need a moment to readjust to darkness. There was a time when I would have closed my eyes instinctually.

Cries go up from the other prisoners, high-pitched keening

and low moans. My voice is not among them and I retreat farther into that stinking black, curling myself into the smallest of balls and pressing the side of my face into the floor.

Rumors have traveled from cell to cell that we will be turned out into the city and left to wander the streets. If such is the case, I have already constructed my plan. The yard at the far end of the zoo where I was housed for months abuts a wooded hill. From my pen I could not see if more woods lay behind it, placing our location at the edge of the city, or if this was merely wishful thinking. On winter nights when smells carried especially well, however, I could lift my face and sniff a forest nearby. This is the direction I will take in long, loping strides if we are set free.

Tonight, I sleep fitfully, the exploding shell a grim reminder of what it would mean to die in confinement. In my sleep I near the crest of the hill while the city falls away behind me. My legs churn on the cell's floor as I dream that pavement transforms into earth underfoot, late fall into winter, and my feet kick up the icy dust of snow. From the top of the hill I can see only forest, rising from black, fragrant soil. The voices of my pack are clear and carry across the winter silence. The sound of my own relieved cries awakens me.

It has been days since they fed us, and my eyesight grows dimmer. I am half of what I was, and would be incapable of running between trees at night. My instincts are dulled, and I would be left behind with the oldest and weakest to pick over the remains from the successful hunts of others. My coat is matted and dull.

Several nights ago, when the moon was full, there was a break-out. An elephant with a massive trunk and feet like tree stumps battered down her door. *I'm free, I'm free*, she trumpeted loudly through the yard, lumbering in jubilant circles.

I saw her, large as a cliff's side, move past my cell and take off running in the direction of the city.

The shelling started in earnest when she left, and I retreated to my familiar place in the far corner. I could hear the shouts of men in the distance and her battle cry as she thundered past burned-out cars and houses in the almost abandoned city.

I'm free, she screamed, communicating at once her fervent desire for things I have never seen: the moist heat of India, the unfurling of crimson flowers underfoot.

It was said later that the mortar which stayed her exploded in a crown of pure red light, and that she bellowed as she fell to her knees. I think I know the exact moment of her collapse. The night had become suddenly quiet, as if all men had frozen in horror at their handiwork. When she fell, the snowmelt that had pooled in the corner of my cell quivered for a moment and went still.

It was said that the harried defenders of the city had sent their best sniper, under fear of more shelling or sniping from the other side. That he had crept as close as he dared, from the body of one abandoned car to another, hiding behind collapsing walls and other debris. He had fired his old rifle time after time, her thick hide absorbing the bullets but never admitting them fully to where they could zigzag through her insides and do their work. It was said that, instead, she bled to death in the street. I have heard that she lies there still, her carcass decomposing on the concrete by day, freezing by night. They say that she is too large to move.

The lines of confrontation are drawn and redrawn nightly.

Sometimes they lie above our yard, sometimes below. Sometimes they stretch to the far northern suburbs of the empty city. But she seems the centerpiece to their battles, a forlorn monument. Buildings are reduced to heaps of dust around her, yet she is a constant, a point indicated in red on aerial maps.

It is the idea that she decomposes here in the city that enrages me in the prison of my cell. I, who never asked anything but to die in the wood or against the white stone that marked the southern extent of our wanderings, my body barely distinguishable from it on moonlit nights. To be stripped down to the clean white of my bones and teeth, with not a piece of flesh left. And to be scattered like dry sticks.

My only hope is the abandoned dogs which roam the city. My distant brothers, they have formed packs that rove by night. I hear them howling in the distance, and raise my head to join their chorus.

Some nights I dream a strange sort of memory. I dream that I am man and shudder from my straw bed on the floor.

Last night, for example, after the shell exploded in the yard, I slept fitfully and dreamed of a warm cave in which my own moist breath had drawn patterns on the walls in lichen shades of green.

There was a woman, some woman I must have previously known, who came into the crawl space and lay beside me. She curled around me and slept. Later, in the darkness of that fragrant space, she arched above me, her body ghostly white. Her hair was a black motion which I caught in my human hands and held up like skeins of wool. The voice that made the inside of the hill vibrate was my own. It wed with hers, our faces raised and pressed against one another, and rose from the cave like smoke and was carried downwind.

When the hunters entered the cave, they killed our pups. Small and blind, the little ones cried out in fright and were bludgeoned one by one. My woman's screams were wild and inconsolable and I saw her leap at one, teeth bared in the light of their torch. Her black hair sailed like a river behind her. The bullet that pierced her chest passed through her entirely and ricocheted from one stony corner of that space to another. In the dream I chased its metallic sound in futility, sniffing out its blood-red tip, from one end to the other, over the twitching bodies of our young.

I am not man, am glad not to be man, I howled repeatedly as the bullet slowed and stilled. The hunters caught me by and by. They placed coarse ropes around my neck and led me out into the snow. Blood ran like a hot river from the cave, and between my feet.

This morning I wake to the sound of that bullet, the steady ricochet as it traverses space. I am weeping as I open my eyes to find the morning silent, save for the steady fall of drops from a knifelike icicle hanging overhead.

I start my pacing again. Still no one feeds us.

The original caretakers of the zoo were not bad types, though they were my jailers. I remember one particularly well, who would sit beyond the confines of my yard and watch me lope the pasture, up and down. He had wire-rimmed glasses and spent his time scribbling in a notebook.

When he approached the fence I would draw near, lowering my head at his voice. I did not know what he was saying and am still thankful that I cannot communicate in his ugly language. But it was the tone and not the words that I understood in the confusion of my first weeks in confinement.

He never fed me, only watched.

Frequently I would return his stare as he dropped to a sitting position outside the fence. I garnered from a note of longing that we were both far from home, and when I drew close enough to see his eyes, their reflections confirmed it. There were high passes inaccessible by man in the wintertime, and the low-pitched lapping from a dozen bent wolves' heads as they drank beside some melted creek.

In summer he would sometimes bring his young, who gamboled on the path outside the fence and considered me with astonished expressions. They would lean close to the fence until he shooed them gently away and returned to his jotting down of data. I would find a patch of shade and watch him with unblinking eyes, a strange truce declared between us.

After the war started, days went by in which he and others protected us from the city's starving citizens. They came to the gates of the zoo brandishing guns and butcher knives and we could hear their hungry voices. In truth, certain cages were emptied to keep the mob at bay. I was never sure which ones.

Then he disappeared.

The city emptied out, the populace trickling like water through some ripped seam. Many of the animals went mad, pacing in their cages, listening to the scream of falling shells. Several of the devices fell within the zoo, bringing down entire buildings. A whole band of monkeys was eliminated early on, nothing left of them and the trees from which they had swung except smoking ash. Others were luckier. The wire netting which kept in the eagles was ripped apart by the same shell, journeying to its target. Except for a few singed tail feathers, they were unscathed and were able to fly away. The rest of the zoo watched in cautious admiration as they pierced the sky, faded to small black dots on the horizon, and disappeared.

The worst, of course, was when a shell fell and injured but did not kill. An animal would lie wounded for hours, cries growing weaker as day and night wore on. It was from listening to them that most of the other animals went mad. Not me. I have managed to hold on to my senses this far, the memory of my wood sustaining me.

Sometimes soldiers from the city, in positions nearby, cannot stand the screams of the wounded. They track the noises to our zoo and with a few violent discharges of their weapons put an end to the misery. It happened that I saw one of them once, the night the lion's cage was hit. He stole into the zoo in the early morning hours, face smeared with dirt so that he would melt into the city's shadows. He discharged a round into the cage, and there followed a thick silence. I sank onto my haunches and waited, resting my chin on my paws. On his way out he passed my cage, but did not look at me. I could tell from the slickness of his face that he was weeping.

I know it is only a matter of time before they go from cage to cage, distributing bullets like medicine. But I have not yet given up on the idea of my hill, and I spend my hours pacing in expectation.

The men who come sporadically now to feed us are strangers. Different ones each time.

The meat which they bring me this afternoon is stringy and old. It is the first meal I have had in days. It falls through the bars with a thud, a fine coating of dirt immediately covering it. But I am not discriminating and finish in three swallows, immediately longing for more.

The sounds of eating and cries of relief go up from other cages.

At one time I would have turned my nose up at the morsels now lying in my stomach, but I do not even remember anymore what it means to hunt fresh meat. I might not know what to do if a roe deer threaded through trees below me. In the cage my legs have grown weak.

And then it happens.

I hear the turning of a key and the door to my cell is left open. I hear footsteps as someone recedes, passing from one cage to the next and opening all the doors. I blink for a moment at the shock of it and, head down, nose hesitantly toward the door. Other animals are approaching the yard, a dozen noses and snouts peering cautiously out of captivity. Slowly we assemble, looking dazedly at one another, and move in one numb herd to the zoo's entrance. The road beyond, which leads into the city, is deserted, and smoke rises in lazy wisps in the distance.

We begin our march, still looking around in some confusion. We are alone, but sense that the men who have set us free have not disappeared entirely. I can feel them looking out at us from the glassless windows of skeletal houses and from cracks in piles of rubble.

Too late, I remember my plan, and the yard and the hill. I stop and turn, weaving my way backwards, against the flow of the slowly moving procession. I break into a run, the rhythmic sound of my paws against the pavement comforting. I will run the perimeter of the zoo until I find my hill. I will surge to its top in a few bounds. When I reach the top, I will know if return is possible.

"Hey you!" someone shouts, and a shot goes up overhead.

I pay no attention. There are strange whines coming from my mouth.

"Stop!" And something whizzes by my ear. It burns like fire. I do not turn around but, feeling the blood start down my face, I stop.

The realization that I can understand them comes as a shock. Have I lived in such proximity to them that I know their language? I turn, holding a hand to my ear, and blink rapidly.

"Get on your knees, you son of a bitch!" They are screaming at me now. The hill flickers in the distance behind me, green and enticing. I come so close to imagining the spring of earth beneath my feet that tears gather in the corners of my eyes.

But I do not sink to my knees. I am done with their games and walk boldly upright toward them. I remove my cracked eyeglasses and throw them onto the road. They make a tinkling sound as they shatter completely.

"Get down!" the voice threatens, but I pay no attention.

"I am not man and am glad not to be man!" I shout. I cannot see their expressions, but sense their outlines tense in surprise. My ears pick up the catch of their weapons, and suddenly I turn and run away from them. Toward the hill and the wood. Toward the den where the dark-haired woman is keeping watch over our phantom young.

The bullets pass like a horizontal gray sleet and I run beyond them, fleeter than any wolf they have ever seen. When I fall, I am still running.

Passage

IN THE DREAM Ivan is lying on his back in a river, completely submerged except for his face. The water is freezing and he imagines the jagged formation of ice in his bloodstream. It is dawn and he cannot remember how long he has been here, looking at the shivering trees, at his powdery breath that hovers over him in clouds before fading into the white winter sky.

He knows that initially he had fought against the quiet overtaking his limbs. He remembers that he was chased here, his bullet-riddled legs moving with surprising agility. At first his blood had poured into the water. It had hovered in a pink cloud around his body and he had watched it dissipate in seconds.

In the dream he shakes his head. *That isn't right.* It had been dark when he sat down in the water. It was too dark to see but he knew the bleeding had slowed from the bland taste of the water, which was no longer threaded with the heavy, sweet smell of blood.

He had lain back, collapsing into the frozen, silent world, a searing pain in his ears. He was waiting, and then dawn came.

Queens was too noisy for Ivan and his younger brother, and the sounds of the street and the smells of Mexican, Chinese, and Lebanese food filled their room on hot summer nights. After the silence of their Adriatic island, the neighborhood's exotic chaos was overwhelming.

"I can't fucking stand it," Pero would tell him, near tears, remembering home.

The war, Ivan realized in those moments, would most certainly have killed his brother. "If we close the window, we'll suffocate," he would point out in a tone that sounded reasonable to him.

And Pero would turn his face to the wall.

Their uncle, who owned a restaurant, had helped to arrange their papers. After a month, he took Ivan aside. "You're a hard worker," he told him, "but your brother is a nightmare." Ivan was promoted to waiting tables, while Pero stayed in the kitchen, his face resentful and perspiring from the clouds of steam that rose from the dishwasher.

Their uncle was an alcoholic who claimed a hard life and a wife who did not understand him. He would come to the brothers' tiny Astoria apartment, a bottle of something tucked into his pocket. Sitting on their only chair, legs flung out in front of him, he would unscrew the bottle as he began speaking.

"It's like the life of a sailor," he would tell them contemplatively, offering the bottle to them. "You never achieve total happiness on either land or water. You'll never be completely happy here, but you wouldn't be there, either."

Pero would curl into a ball on his bed and pull the pillow over his ears. When his uncle fell asleep, Ivan would take the bottle away so that it would not slip out of his hand and crash to the floor, disturbing the Korean family that lived below them.

One night, he placed the thick bottle in the sink, and when it reverberated against the metal, his uncle stirred behind him in his chair. Ivan turned and saw his uncle staring with a scowl at Pero's sleeping back. "It's because you didn't have a father around. Your mother spoiled him and now look." His watery eyes turned on Ivan. "You were just a kid then. Do you remember?"

Ivan did not answer. He bent to clear the overflowing ashtray.

His uncle stretched out on Ivan's bed, continuing to talk. " . . . just a kid, and when we heard the news we ran down to your mother's place, but she already knew . . ." Ivan lay on the bed beside Pero and closed his eyes. *Old man*, he thought, *go to sleep or get out.*

But his uncle rose again and poured a philosophical four fingers from another bottle secreted somewhere in the folds of his coat. Ivan tried to tune him out. He thought about the next day at work and whether he would have to iron his pants. He thought about one of the waitresses, an American girl with big breasts who wore fluffy sweaters to work before changing into a tight black skirt and white blouse. Angora, she had told him shyly in the storeroom once, letting him touch the softness of her sleeve.

". . . died the way our grandfathers did, Ivan, the way we were all meant to go . . . at sea . . ."

"It was an accident," Ivan said sharply, his eyes flying open. He could feel Pero groan soundlessly beside him. "A concussion and he was dead before they got back to port."

". . . the way we were all meant to," his uncle continued. "Not here in fucking America. Not in Astoria . . . left your mother all alone. And you were so little, Ivan, and Pero just a baby, and I knew I had to get out. Do you know that feeling, when you know you're going to die? You can see the beginning, middle, and end from where you sit and you have to move . . ." And he began suddenly to sing, his drunken voice warbling through the tiny apartment. "Sing with me, Ivan," he insisted. Ivan imagined hitting him and watching blood trickle from his cut lip.

His uncle was saying something about the war, about Ivan having to leave because of Pero. "You would never have left," he told him. "You had the right to stay." And suddenly he was asleep, snoring heavily. Ivan dreaded having to rouse him in the morning.

"I didn't have the right to stay, is that it?" Pero muttered next to him in the bed.

"Shut up and go to sleep," he told his brother. But their uncle's words hung above him in the room, like a cloud of noxious smoke that even sleep did not drive away.

"He'll never survive," their mother had told Ivan months before, her face white and pinched. "You know he won't."

The mobilization orders had come that morning.

"You know he won't," she repeated. "What are we going to do?"

"I'll handle it," he told her. And he did, talking to the people he knew on the draft board. He pushed his brother's name back two rotations.

"I wouldn't do this for just anybody," the man on the board had said, pocketing the hundred-deutsche-mark note. "What the hell are you afraid of anyway? It's barely war anymore. It certainly isn't what you saw."

But Ivan had only glowered at him.

What he had seen was a defensive that had driven the Serbs back, and how they had entered a town after a massacre. They had spent a day picking up the dead and laying them on a piece of plastic sheeting to await burial. He had found the bodies of three girls behind a barn. Sisters, as he later found out, and he had placed them side by side on the sheeting. He had carried them, without realizing, in order of age.

The eldest had been dark-haired, a little younger than his own twenty years, he guessed. The middle sister had been lighter, and had a bland face. He remembered that he had needed to pry them out of each other's arms to transport them to the grave. The youngest had been blond, a little girl of about six years old, and he had watched her surprised face as he carried her.

"Just take his name off," he told the man.

Word got out and sped across the island with the ferocity of a wildfire. Their neighbor, whose son had been in Ivan's unit and was killed at the start of the war, stopped talking to them altogether.

"We've got to get him out," their mother persisted. "I nearly lost one son, I'm not about to lose the other."

Pero's face had reddened as he walked out of the room. But not before Ivan saw something else in his face, a slow blossoming of fear.

"He's scared to stay, and he's scared to go alone," their mother said.

And Ivan noticed that his brother had not insisted, as other young men might, that he could fight his own battles. And he was suddenly ashamed of the fact that he had noticed, and that this thought had filled him with a certain calculating coldness.

"You've got to get him out," their mother told Ivan.

The evening before they left the island, they had each taken a handful of pebbles from the town's beach. Ivan had scooped them up randomly and wrapped them in his handkerchief, squeezing the salt water from the edges with his thumb and forefinger. Pero had gathered them deliberately, selecting smooth white stones, pieces of fractured coral, and spiral shells. He placed them, one by one, in his pocket with Ivan standing behind him on the beach in a white T-shirt, silhouetted against the pine forest.

On the way home, they had stopped at their grandmother's house. Nearly blind, she had held her palm to each man's forehead and begun to cry. The brothers shifted wordlessly from foot to foot. They looked at one another, each wondering the same thing. *Are a blind man's tears of the same substance as a seeing man's?* And when they bent to kiss her cheeks, she whispered to each one in turn. To Pero she said, "Ivan, watch over your younger brother. He's not as strong as you."

In Ivan's ear she whispered, "My child, your brother's not right since the war. But listen to him always, my little Pero."

On the ride home, Pero shouted at his brother over the groan of the motorcycle. "What did she say to you?"

And Ivan shrugged, turning sideways so that his brother could see his white, straight teeth. He answered but his voice was drowned out by the wind.

When the plane took off, Pero removed the last piece of fried bread their mother had packed for them from a napkin that was translucent with oil. Ivan sat beside him in the aisle seat with his eyes shut. Pero knew his brother was not asleep and he watched him thoughtfully as he crumpled the napkin and chewed.

The airplane rose higher, burying itself in a white sky, and Pero saw that the green-and-brown land underneath was erased. His heart began to beat quickly as a bird's. He imagined himself flying parallel to the plane, lifted suddenly on gusts of wind and diving in the intervals.

Ivan thought that he could hear the beating of his brother's heart. It seemed to be carving out a hole in his upper arm. He shifted and imagined the land fading as if he were in his boat leaving shore. *On a cloudy day, the land surrounds you and then, suddenly, ebbs. As if a curtain of smoke had suddenly descended, as if you have passed into another place completely.*

The American waitress's name was Beth and she had long brown hair that she wore in a French braid. Ivan had been shy around her at first, ashamed of his clumsy English, which was passable when taking orders but rapidly deteriorated in her vicinity. He would lift his eyes from his order pad to find her watching him from across the room. When they brushed by each other, he could not resist the temptation to touch her and let his fingertips graze her back.

Months went by before they spoke. One day, walking to the restaurant from the subway station, he saw her ahead of him, hands shoved into the pockets of her coat. She was oblivious to his presence and he did not hurry to catch up with her. Rounding the corner, she slipped on a patch of ice and fell with a cry.

He broke into a jog, reaching her side as she massaged her ankle with a grimace. Wordlessly, he offered her his hand and helped her to her feet.

"Damn!" she muttered, standing on one foot. "I think I sprained it."

His uncle gave him the car keys to drive her to the hospital for X rays and he sat in the emergency room with her rapidly swelling foot cradled in his lap.

She kept up a steady stream of chatter, telling him about her family and how strange she felt in New York City, having moved from the Midwest. "I can't even imagine what it must be like for you," she said, shaking her head.

"What do you study?" he asked, suddenly. He had heard that she was going to college part-time.

"Teaching."

"I was very bad pupil," he told her, smiling. "And my English is very bad."

"No," she told him, "you just need practice." And she tilted her head to one side and studied him.

One week later she returned to work and started taking her meal with him in the kitchen. He asked her whether she would like to go to a movie with him, and she nodded her head. "Sure, Ivan, that would be fun."

He liked the way she said his name, careful to pronounce it correctly. Most Americans made the *I* long, making his name sound like a subject and a verb. "I van," they would tell him, and the first time he had been confused, and had almost consulted a dictionary for the meaning of the verb "to van." But she said it neatly, sparely.

She placed her plate in the sink and returned to work, unaware of Pero scowling at her nearby. Ivan looked after her with a bemused expression.

"I thought you didn't like American girls," Pero said after she had gone. The banging of dishes brought Ivan out of his reverie.

Ivan frowned. "Don't start with me."

"You said they were loud and chewed too much gum," he continued.

"She isn't loud and she doesn't chew gum."

Pero turned his back and lifted the side of the industrial washer to slide out a tray of dishes, and Ivan turned on his heel to leave the kitchen. When he cleared the door, he heard a glass being thrown against it, shattering on the floor.

When Pero was five, he had an overwhelming fear of sea urchins. He would spend hours sitting on a rock watching their coal-black bodies beneath the surface of the water. He would drop white pebbles into the water, watching them drift slowly downward and nestle between the urchins' spines, but he refused to pick his way between them into the sea.

The other boys, who dove from rocks and splashed happily in the water, made fun of him. They were solid, brown-skinned boys who fell asleep during school after long nights spent fishing in their fathers' boats. Only rarely would they make a misstep and come up howling, the black needles embedded beneath the surface of the skin.

In order for Pero to swim, Ivan had to clear a path for him by gently prying the urchins from the rock by hand and throwing them back into the water at a safe distance. Only then would Pero clamber down from his rock, taking Ivan's hand, and ease himself into the water. Once submerged, he swam like a fish, and the boys would have contests to see who could dive deeper and stay under longer.

Ivan was able to hold his breath for a full minute, scrabbling around the bottom, watching the legs of the other boys shining through the ceiling of water above him. Pero's legs were always the smallest and the whitest.

Pero could hold his breath for surprisingly long, hands and legs working furiously to prevent himself from rising to the surface. But once he had stayed down so long that his brother began to grow nervous and dove to find him drifting, face downward, on the bottom. Panic had risen in Ivan's throat and he grabbed his brother's arm, his legs kicking furiously until they reached the air. Pero's face had been ashen and the other boys had helped drag him back onto a rock.

Ivan had screamed and pummeled his brother's chest while one of the other boys ran for help, and Pero had finally choked, turning his head to the side to let a stream of water spill from his mouth onto the rock. But when his eyes opened, they were triumphant. "I stayed down longer," he told his brother in a raw whisper as Ivan knelt above him, so relieved that he had started to cry.

As their first year in America passed, it was the memory of little things that made Ivan melancholy. At the end of summer, he would wake up having dreamed of the pale yellow color of figs. The insides were red and as sweet as honey. In winter, it was the pitch of the *bura*, the cold northerly wind that howled around his mother's stone house. New York's congested skyline blocked out the light, and he also thought wistfully of the sun that baked his island like a loaf of bread.

But there were other memories. They crept into his dreams and left him shivering and bloody in a winter stream. So that when Pero felt nostalgic, Ivan was unsympathetic. "*Što je, tu je,*" he would tell his brother. "This is the way things are."

"I am tired of listening to you!" Pero shouted the night Ivan returned home from his date with Beth. They had gone to a movie and he had walked her home before taking the N train back to their apartment. She had been sweet and warm on the front steps of her building, opening her coat to allow his hands to creep around her waist and touch her back. Her kiss had been soft and its taste had lingered in his mouth.

At his brother's words another, bitter taste replaced it. "And I am tired of taking care of you," Ivan shouted back.

The Koreans downstairs were silent for a moment before they began to move around in their apartment again.

Pero stumbled past him and out the front door. "I'm going out."

"Put on your coat!" Ivan barked at him, but his brother ignored him and Ivan heard the stairs in the hallway shake as Pero descended them angrily.

Going to the window, he saw the streak of his brother's white shirt as Pero ran down the street. He sighed, watching him turn a corner, and then sat down to finish writing the letter he had started to their mother. He spent several minutes looking at it, chewing the end of the pen. "We are well and healthy," he wrote to her.

In some of Ivan's dreams, his brother is five years old and sitting on a bank beside the river. "Ivan," he calls out, shivering. "Ivan, I'm ready to go."

But he cannot rise from the water, nor can he respond. The iciness has immobilized him. He can see the men creeping up from the woods behind his brother and he aches for his voice. He aches to be able to jump to his feet and hoist his brother into his arms and run. But the weight on his body is overwhelming.

He watches the men signal to each other and draw their knives. In the dream, he begins to whimper. His brother's body falls over him, into the river. It is pale and bloodless under the water.

He began to spend the nights at Beth's apartment, the two of them stumbling to her street almost drunkenly after their long shift. She had a large orange cat that curled up by their heads in the bed. In her apartment, he never had his river dreams. He dreamed only that he was being suffocated by cotton, opening his eyes to find the cat on his chest.

Pero was barely speaking to him now, not even looking up

when he arrived at work in the mornings, until one day he did not show up at all.

Their uncle threw up his hands in disgust.

"I'll go get him," Ivan told him. "We'll be right back."

The door to the apartment was unlocked and he found Pero sitting underneath the window with a bottle. *"Brate,"* Pero said, his voice dripping with saccharine warmth. "Brother. So nice to see you again."

"You're going to work," Ivan told him, even then realizing that his brother would not be able to make the trip, much less work his shift. "What the hell is wrong with you?"

"I'm going back home."

"Bullshit." Ivan rubbed his eyes, sitting down on the bed.

"I will," he insisted, his eyes suddenly sober. "What do I have to be afraid of? I'm going to die faster here."

And Ivan had stared at him angrily. "I came because of you."

"Come back with me, then."

He shook his head slowly. No.

Inside the terminal, they embrace awkwardly. Pero looks down at his shoes and then up at his brother. "Don't you long for your home?"

And Ivan thinks of his fishing boat, the little Tomos motor leaving a white wake like a plane writing letters in the sky. On hot days, they would thread through the maze of islands. He would navigate between them and Pero would let his legs trail in the water. And moonless nights were so black that the Milky Way actually shone in the dark sea. It had been months since he had seen a star in New York.

But he pushes the thought away and shakes his head. A vision of his brother's body on plastic sheeting rises up in his mind and he blinks back tears.

After Pero's plane takes off, Ivan stands at one of the airport's large glass windows, fists shoved into his pockets. He cannot be certain which is his brother's plane, so he picks one at random to watch. Its wings tilt in the blue sky like a boat in rough seas, but it leaves no trace of a wake.

The Angled
City

N. HAS DEVELOPED a code of conduct which requires his fierce attention. He does not fire at men in tan coats, red-haired women, or groups of three. He shoots cats for lack of better targets, but considers dogs a waste of his time and skill. And after wedging the butt of his post-lunch cigarette filter-first into the cinder-block wall by his shoulder, he might fire five shots in quick succession even if nothing moves in the space below. The red point of light should still be glowing at the end of his cigarette when he lowers the rifle. If not, he will swear softly, tap out another from the pack, and start again.

Boredom dictates his principles, and in deference to that

mother of idle invention he reverses them on Wednesdays, spending a day shooting only at those targets he has previously renounced.

He moves from building to building, changing position and floor regularly, sometimes obeying sporadic orders, sometimes following his own whims. In the beginning he spent several miserable weeks on a forested mountain above the city, determining almost immediately his aversion to sitting with his back against the rough bark of pine trees. Off the lines in those weeks, he would awaken in a cot at the base camp with his hair glued to the pillow and the smell of tree resin sharp in his nostrils. And when home on leave, his wife made no end of fuss as she scrubbed the sap from his jacket and boiled a pan of water, hoping to melt it away.

But now he is back in his element, positioned in an abandoned apartment building in the foothills, directly facing the city below. It is part of a series of socialist buildings, all identical and of shoddy construction. The sameness comforts him with its stifling and squalid precision, a block of strategically placed mirrors that could stretch onward to gray infinity.

He remembers this building without being able to place it exactly. This is the general rule for all the buildings in the city, whose faces have undergone sudden and drastic surgery during the war. Often the positioning of a window or a space of flaked paint is enough to trigger a feeling of uneasy recognition. Like as not, this feeling will be replaced by the realization that he has not actually seen the building in any previous incarnation.

All the same, the building strikes him as one he should remember. Perhaps a high school girlfriend lived here and they once sat together on the steps as he tried to move his hand to the tempting no-man's-land beneath her bra. Or maybe he had visited it earlier on a pilgrimage to some distant and aged aunt. He had memories of a hundred of the city's buildings, of visits with his mother to anonymous elderly women. Their kitchens all turned out identical cakes and juices of cloying sweetness and their faces faded into the same gray mass of cigarettes and coffee-scented gossip.

The conversations float to him over the space of years, wiped down to the same gum color. There was always some son who had fled to Germany, a husband who had followed his dick but not his good sense into another woman's bed. And then the merciful sight of his mother as she rose and snapped her handbag shut. *No, we really must be going now.* And the feel of her hand on his shoulder as they walked to the stop and caught the bus back to the distant suburbs.

Yesterday he had explained his system to the giant who stood in position at the other window. They had been strangers until a few days ago. The man's unruly black whiskers and mouth of broken teeth, not to mention the blunted country accent, made N. uneasy, but he was so unaccustomed to company that words poured forth in an unstoppable stream. The man, whom N. had privately nicknamed Fang, only stared at him in response, the broken teeth giving him a look of added astonishment.

"You've got to be fucking kidding me," Fang said, bursting into laughter so hard that he dropped to the concrete floor and slapped it repeatedly with a meaty palm.

And N. looked at him, blinking in surprise. *He's just a peasant*, he finally told himself. *Of course he wouldn't understand*. Fang came from a hamlet unmarked on any map, more used to gutting pigs and rolling them into sausage than to pissing indoors. In fact, he relieved himself wherever it struck his fancy in the huge abandoned building, marking his territory like a dog. Not even like a dog, N. had to correct himself, because a dog would not sleep near his own shit. And N. had spent several miserable evenings downwind of whatever room Fang had designated as toilet for that day, while the fat man snored contentedly in another corner.

More adept at emptying bottles of brandy than hitting his targets, Fang used his gun only marginally well. In the days they had shared the post, N. noticed a distinct curve in Fang's marksmanship. Within the first quarter bottle his aim improved slightly, before steadily worsening. By the end of the half bottle, he would shoot at birds in flight, tree branches, and, on one notable occasion, the ceiling.

"Don't you have a system?" N. asked disdainfully when the man's laughter had subsided to an occasional hiccup.

Fang shook his head in amusement. "I just shoot. The more the better. I'm a simple man and I have a simple system."

And N. turned his back in silence.

"You city boys," Fang said, shaking his head and rising to his feet. He brushed off the seat of his pants. "All the same shit."

Or maybe it had been his piano teacher. She had lived on a hill in the outskirts. A cousin or ex-wife of one of his father's colleagues, she had given him lessons at a discount. He remembers walking to her apartment under duress, piano music dog-eared and crumpled in his school bag.

She was young, with long legs and inexpertly dyed blond hair. The apartment was small and filled with heavy wooden furniture. Before each practice, she brought him a glass of water which she set on a coaster on the upright piano. In summer, water condensed in a veil of pearl-like drops, and he would watch them gather through some strange magnetic attraction and fall. To demonstrate how his arms should be held straight, she would move behind him and put a hand on each wrist. He remembers closing his eyes as her breasts grazed his shoulder and the back of his neck.

She had smelled of perspiration and scented powder. His father always moved a little too close when greeting her, and his mother sniffed over the appliances in her apartment. "Connections," she'd mutter once out of earshot. "That woman has connections."

N. now looks urgently around the gutted apartment, trying to match it with hers. He remembers that there were two windows in her living room, approximately one meter apart, and that the parquet had the same herringbone pattern. One wall, less destroyed than the others, still bears paint and the traces of former times: tiny black nail holes and scuff marks form a perfect rectangle where a picture once hung. Had she had a picture there? He seemed to remember a picture of the sea and a boat. He closes his eyes and imagines the room as it had looked then. When he opens his eyes, the bare cinder blocks grin back, as plain and ridiculous as bone. The rectangle of pale color could be a trick of the light that filters in through the windows. He shakes his head. He cannot be sure.

At the end of the first week in the apartment, he had twenty-three hits. Excellent, even by his own demanding standards. He and Fang called them out to each other, and he noted with satisfaction that the other man was feeling the strain. Fang had already lied twice, claiming hits when people had clearly scurried out of view.

N. only smiled. "What aim," he commented dryly after the second shot. "What superb control."

When Fang spat on the floor and left the apartment for the entire afternoon, N. welcomed the chance to return to the precision of his game.

Through his scope he can see a man, carrying a plastic container of water on his shoulder, look out into the intersection below. The intersection is N.'s favorite because of its challenging angle. The buildings on either side provide a blind, leaving only the very center of the street exposed. The time in which to make a hit is so short that it demands all his concentration. His code complicates things further, because the time it takes him to rule out tan coats, red hair, and groups of three could be critical.

Every few minutes he spots the man peeking around the corner of a building, deciding whether to come out.

"Come on," N. tells him, never removing his eye from the scope. "Come on."

The man emerges, zigzagging across the intersection. He lumbers under the weight of the water and N. waits until he is in the center of the street before firing. The bullet shoots out like an electrical charge, piercing the plastic container and the man's head. Though he is too far to see the color of the water emptying, he imagines it swirling in pink circles on the pavement below.

When Fang returns some time later, N. is smoking and reading an old newspaper. The fat man offers him the clear bottle under his arm. It tastes like fire, but N. drinks from it in giant gulps. "Nothing like homemade," he says casually, replacing the cap and handing the bottle back.

That night he leaves Fang sleeping, curled up in blankets in one corner. The smell of alcohol and sweat fills the room, clinging to him like a film of oil. He removes the handgun at his hip as well as his wallet. He stuffs a few rolled-up German marks into the top of his sock and hides his rifle under his blanket, where it looks like a small, bony child.

He pulls on his battered jacket over an unremarkable shirt. A cousin had brought the jacket from Switzerland before the war, and it was stuffed with high-quality down and had detachable sleeves. N. was uncommonly proud of the logo, a Swiss cross.

His heart is hammering in anticipation. It is hard to get in and out of the city, but not impossible, and he has been dreaming about going there for weeks. He wears jeans and is of average height, with close-cropped hair. There is nothing about him that stands out. He is not sure what he plans to do there or what he expects to find, but he can think of nothing else.

The night is thick and dark. Electricity to the district has been cut off for months, and there is no moon. He waits a moment until his eyes grow accustomed to the night and then strikes out.

He is comfortable in the dark, secure on wooded slopes, but here he hurries across open spaces. He can imagine the saline glow of his body through someone's night vision goggles and breaks into a sweat. On several occasions, he ducks behind whatever barrier he can find, thinking he has heard someone behind him. Once he hears the voices of men on guard duty. A hundred meters safely past them and he will know that he has penetrated the dark edges of the city.

The streets seem familiar, and he often stops to run his hands over the rough exteriors of the buildings. There are as many variations of dark as there are of light, and the buildings are a thicker, deader darkness than the rest of the landscape. But as quickly as recognition comes, it recedes, and he proceeds this way into the center of the city: walking, touching one surface after another as if for confirmation, then moving on.

He looks at his watch, careful to cup his right hand around its face before pressing the light. It is 1 a.m. When he lifts his head he hears muffled vibrations like the wheels of a train in the distance or water in ancient pipes, and he moves quickly to press himself against a building. It takes him several moments to realize that the sounds are music and singing, so incongruous are they in the immobile and deserted street.

It seems that it has been years since he has heard those sounds, and he tracks them like a dog following a scent, determining that they come from the cellar of an apartment building across the street. He drops to his knees outside the building, hoping to find a window at the level of the rubble-strewn pavement through which to see. But the windows are covered from the inside with paper. He reaches through a grille and places his palm on the dust-covered glass. The sounds grow louder and the window reverberates under his hand.

Rising, he gropes his way along the wall until he finds the doors. He pushes through them into a hallway and descends the barely lit stairs in front of him. At the bottom, he pushes past another set of doors into a subterranean bar lit by candles and filled with smoke so thick it presses against his skin like velvet.

No one notices his arrival, and the door closes behind him with a sigh.

A short time later, he finds himself seated at one of the low tables, a drink in front of him. He does not know who ordered it or whether it simply appeared, but he drinks deeply without noticing the taste and a moment later there is another full glass in its place.

Large, raucous groups surround him, and he finds himself part of one conversation and then another, the odd man sent from team to team, absorbed and reabsorbed as if in a strange dance.

The people are of all ages, men and women. Some are already drunk, leaning heavily against each other. A song starts in one corner of the room and is picked up in another, undergoing a process of mutation by which few notes are sung in unison or on key, but roll like soft thunder.

"No going home until morning," the girl on his left says, squeezing his arm. The candlelight makes her angular face glow like mother-of-pearl. She peers into his face. "You're new? I don't recognize you."

His mouth goes dry, but he smiles and leans close to her ear. "I'm just here on vacation. Lovely city."

And she laughs, bending at the waist. When she straightens, he sees that tears are sliding from her eyes in straight vertical tracks. He cannot tell if she is drunk or just easily amused.

He could swear that he has spotted several people he knows. Childhood playmates, girlfriends, even the blond piano teacher, who he is sure is sitting in the corner on someone's lap and does not appear to have aged a day. But she seems to avoid looking in his direction, and he is not so sure of her identity after all.

Morning comes and they all pile into the street. He has the sense that he has been in the underground bar for days. He stands mutely as people stumble in different directions and call out their goodbyes. The girl who had sat beside him emerges from the building and places a hand on his shoulder.

"Enjoy your vacation," she tells him with a steady grin. Something in his stomach jumps, and for a moment he is sure that she has guessed his identity. In the light he can now see a vertical scar which starts at her eye and stretches to her chin. The tears of the previous night had merely followed that well-worn groove. He wants to touch it with his thumb, to bend her neck backward with a ferocious kiss and stretch his tongue so far that it would lap the wet tissue of her lungs. But she moves away from him and he watches her disappear around a corner.

It occurs to him that the city has become a patchwork of angles and disappearances, and he spends the next hours wandering the streets. He stops at intervals to read the only functioning newspaper, which cannot be distributed as in prewar days but is instead posted in bulletin form on walls and poles. He catches sight of buildings which he recognizes from a distance, only to have them fade into strangeness and anonymity upon approach.

Walking toward one such building—*was it his grade school?*— he reaches the intersection, almost stepping unwittingly out into the line of fire before someone grabs his collar from behind.

"Careful," the voice hisses in his ear. "You've got to move fast when you go. Those fuckers are just sitting and waiting."

The words reach N. through an underwater cloud of silt. He had not recognized the intersection from this perspective.

The stranger suddenly bolts past him in a streak of speed and light. N. sees, for a split second, his face in profile and freezes.

"Wait!" N. shouts. But the man runs through the intersection as if he did not hear him. There are several cracks from a rifle, but he passes through unscathed, not stopping on the other side but melting immediately behind the next block.

N. stands there blinking furiously, and then turns blindly in the opposite direction.

Back at the apartment post that night Fang is snoring loudly, and it seems to N. as if he has never been away, as if the past twenty-four hours are an imaginary loop which closes the minute he enters the stuffy room. His rifle still lies beneath the blanket and he shoves it aside to make room to sleep.

In the morning he wakes to find Fang standing against the far wall, staring at him. "We're supposed to move later today," the man tells him. "They came yesterday and I told them you were only gone a half hour."

N. rises and stretches. He has a cigarette before sliding out the rifle and taking up position by the window.

"I hope she's got tits like melons," Fang muttered behind him. "A whole day's worth."

N. puts his eye against the scope, feeling the familiar touch of slender metal on his brow, and smiles. "Like basketballs," he murmurs. He hears the other man sigh behind him and take up position at the other window.

Not even the wind moves through the intersection below. N. scans the periphery, sweeping from one side to the other. At first the movement is so slight he almost misses it. But several minutes later he sees it again, just the barest hint of something, like hair in a barely existent breeze.

"I'm moving now," Fang says behind him. "You come when you're ready." N. hears the footfalls fade behind him, and the sound of Fang's coughing as he descends the stairwell, but he does not take his eye from the scope. There it is again. The sensation of fluttering toward the left side of the intersection, as if promising the arrival of something more significant.

"Come on." N. hears his own voice echo in the empty apartment.

And the man steps out from behind the wall, not running this time. He walks deliberately into the center of the intersection, coming straight toward N., whose finger trembles on the trigger.

Come on, N. thinks the man mouths. *Come on!*

N. shudders and closes his eyes tightly before opening them again. The regular features, the close-cropped hair. Except for his down jacket, the man is altogether nondescript. The red cross on its breast seems the only point of light in the colorless charcoal space.

Drops of sweat start running through his eyebrows and burning the surface of his eyes.

Maybe the man is his twin, separated at birth, he thinks wildly. Maybe yesterday a piece of his own body broke off in that city, growing arms and legs, and a face that looks remarkably like his. He remembers learning how severed pieces of starfish are able to grow anew. Regeneration.

The man in the fleece jacket is still standing in the intersection, expectantly. The smile on his lips turns derisive and he waves impatiently. N. blinks the sweat from his eyelashes and it drops down his face in cold vertical lines.

The man in the intersection has hatred and resentment written on his face. In that instant both men imagine the same thing: the bull's-eye of the red Swiss cross and the sudden explosion of white feathers from the jacket. The way they would rise and shiver in the air.

N. takes a breath and fires.

The Peacebroker

"TO KNOW US," they had told him, "you must know our habits." He had decided that their main habit was drinking, if not outright drunkenness, a proclivity with which he had little argument.

On his first trip to "the war-torn Balkans," the peacebroker had managed to amass a fine collection of *šljivovica*, the firewater they always supplied at the beginning of meals. They pressed it into his hands in gay paper wrapping or in coffinlike wooden boxes, making his a collection as voluminous as it was varied. There was *šljivovica* from Slavonia, from Posavina, and from a workers' collective outside Belgrade. There were flat circular bottles and cylindrical ones, decorated with pictures of women in

bright peasant costumes and, on one notable occasion, of a benev-
olently grinning Tito. He had quickly become a connoisseur of the
drink, realizing eventually that the smoothest did not in fact come
in fancy industrial packaging, but from someone's private still.

"My father's," they would say, uncapping the glass mineral water bottle in which the homemade brew was invariably presented.
Or, "My brother's. The plums are from his orchard." The pourer
would lean toward him conspiratorially, pouring two fingers into
a glass. And he would throw it back while they watched approv-
ingly. The edges of things would suddenly come into focus.

He returned home with his cadre of bottles and even had several shipped through the diplomatic pouch. In the weeks to come,
far away from the shelling, mass deportations, and summary exe-
cutions, he would fill the glasses of guests at his well-appointed
home with the clear plum fire.

"Authentic, that," he told them proudly. "They drink the stuff
like water."

The men would drain their glasses, careful to keep the muscles of their faces from going rigid. Some had been to the region
themselves, and sampled as many varieties as their host. They
would watch the reactions of other guests with bemused expressions.

Their wives sipped politely, though hardly ever finishing.
Amid a chorus of indulgent chuckles, they would cough delicately
into their hands and comment that it made their eyes tear.

No one ever took a second glass, and, the novelty spent, they
switched to aperitifs more befitting their circumstances. Scotch
for the men, spritzers for the ladies. Choice wines accompanied
their meals.

And he would sit back with a slightly bored expression and consider the refined conversations around him, the half-filled glass bottle atop his mantel incongruous with its exotic lettering. The liquid inside was clear, but gleaming from some wild and hidden flame.

He considered himself quite frankly a step above other Western officials involved in shuttle diplomacy. Theirs was a small and select club, but some members had yet to see the writing on the wall. His own approach was one of hard-learned pragmatism, the lack of which he could only pity in others.

There were two difficult facts he had come to accept over the course of his career. First, war was an inevitable habit of the human race. Second, there was no brotherhood of man.

He found there to be few points of light worldwide: England and certain other Western European countries, Canada, perhaps. America, when he was feeling charitable. The rest was a wasteland. Not that the wasteland could not be fascinating in its own right. Colonialism, though it was fashionable to judge it harshly, had introduced generations of the world's decision makers to something beyond themselves. It had toughened their skins, creating resolute and steadfast men. In a way, he considered himself their true heir, and felt he had little in common with his contemporaries.

Of course, his pragmatic philosophy had taken years to solidify. He had not always been so savvy. He could remember watching *The King and I* as a child. Well into adulthood he remembered Anna stepping off the boat to greet the natives of Siam. They had come to love her, and she had been their bridge to the civilized world.

That naïveté had vanished with his first Africa posting, however. In the middle of revolutions, plagues, and famines, the strains of "Getting to Know You" had played in his head with decreasing frequency. Later, he could not remember at which point they all but stopped, or which pair of suffering eyes had made the diplomatic act degenerate from enthusiasm to rote necessity.

He learned that little of the world was interested in becoming civilized, and even less was worth the effort.

On his second trip to the Balkans, he mastered their jokes.

"To understand us," they had told him, "you must understand our humor."

The inevitable Mujo-Suljo stories about two Bosnian country bumpkins were as widely disseminated as *šljivovica*. He even learned to deliver a punch line or two in their language.

He shared a few of the less bawdy ones with his wife upon his return, but she only looked at him blankly and he grew annoyed. Perhaps the jokes were funny only in the context in which they were told.

Later that night, she turned to him in bed and told him worriedly, "You seem so far away."

And he patted her hand comfortingly, neatly flipped her on her back, and climbed on top. But his mood did not improve and he was glad to be leaving again the next day.

"Can't they find someone else to save the world?" she asked him in the morning.

He hesitated, unsure for a moment whether she was mocking him. "No rest for the wicked, darling," he had told her lightly.

Oh, he understood their humor all right. Black as graveyard dirt.

He had helped negotiate a series of cease-fires early on. "I have your word then?" he had asked the emissary of the Yugoslav People's Army.

"But of course" was the game reply. "We are men of honor."

And no sooner had the ink dried on an agreement than the artillery attacks, airplane bombing, or tank shelling would begin again.

"Really, gentlemen," he had said at one point in exasperation, "why promise something when you can't deliver?" He had even told them the story of the boy who cried wolf.

And they responded with rapt, lupine smiles.

On his third wartime trip, he got to know them further. His interpreter was a tall, lean-limbed woman everyone called Beba who had been a champion ballroom dancer in Belgrade and chain-smoked Marlboro Reds.

"To know us, you must know our soul," one of the analysts he bankrolled said, "and Beba, she's got lots of it."

She was an expert tease, and it took him a number of dinners and receptions at ambassadors' residences to finally corner her in the darkness of a coatroom and put his hand up her skirt.

"Darling," she said with a laugh, and drained the glass, not bothering to push his hand away.

She drank vodka neat, and he watched her Adam's apple bob as she leaned her head back to swallow the contents of her glass. "Do you ever drink *šljivovica*?" he asked her idly.

She burst out laughing. "No, darling!" And moved expertly around him. "*Šljivovica* is for peasants."

He had been a member of a diplomatic mission in Belgrade in the 1980s, and still had a number of friends there. He thought it gave him a singular perspective from which to view the current situation, a point he made frequently to his peers. Back then, people had hardly heard of Sarajevo or Zagreb. For him, Yugoslavia had consisted of the elite Dedinje section of Belgrade, and the odd trip down to the Adriatic coast.

In those early days, he had set his wife up at their residence, where she quickly began ordering maintenance men in the arrangement of furniture. Although it was not their first posting abroad, he had been nervous that she would feel lonely and isolated. But she quickly joined a club of diplomats' wives who took aerobics classes and arranged shopping expeditions to Italy. It was a load off his mind, enabling him to turn his attention to more pressing business, most immediately the cultural attaché's wife. She had been an actress before marrying into the diplomatic service, and was bored silly with her new life.

"Commercials mostly, I'm afraid," she told everyone with charming self-deprecation. "Never a leading lady. Detergent. Yogurt. That sort of thing."

"Unmentionables, more likely," his wife had snorted privately, taking an immediate dislike to her. "Maxi pads. Douches. That sort of thing."

Next, he made a daring move across cultural boundaries. Macina Šapa was Bosnian and a musical specimen particular to the Balkans: turbo-folk diva, decked out in high heels, thick makeup, and an alarming amount of décolleté. She had warbled from one end to the other of the bistro in which he discovered her. She took turns sitting on patrons' laps, and ended each set by blowing kisses to the audience with her brick-red nails and cooing in accented English, "Love you. Love you so much!"

"I am the Yugoslav Edith Piaf," she had insisted. "Only with a different repertoire. And sexier."

But his most memorable liaison in those years had been with a writer-reporter-feminist from Zagreb whose father was a high-ranking Yugoslav army officer, and whose mother had been a guard at a women's prison for political dissidents.

"Lies," she had told him. "Half-truths. The women there were felons."

He had seen the family's dossier but withheld comment.

There was a television spot of her clad in a fashionable suit and high heels, a butterfly in a drab factory courtyard. Her nails were tastefully manicured, and she held up the arm of the woman next to her, a nearsighted *baba* with crooked teeth and a handkerchief covering her hair.

"My sister!" she had proclaimed triumphantly, like a victorious boxer in the ring.

He had not seen any of his former mistresses since returning to the region. The actress was long gone, rumored to have left her diplomat husband for a pair of Russian businessmen. Macina Šapa was still making music, and had become the darling of certain underworld circles he preferred not to explore. The feminist was living abroad and was developing a reputation as an author in the self-help genre.

But he remembered the affinity of his local women for French perfume and cigarettes. He remembered the hungry quality of their embraces, the way they wrapped their legs around him and asked for presents from the duty free.

A decade later and a decade younger than the others, Beba possessed a calculating nature which outshone theirs, and he thrilled to it. She made him feel important and replaceable at the same time. The first time he had taken her to bed, she had teased him relentlessly.

"Would the peacebroker like me to undress now?" she asked, deftly unzipping her dress in one clean movement that reminded him of a magician pulling something furry from his hat.

"My handsome peacebroker," she said, moving toward him with smoky eyes. With her accent, it sounded to him more like "pissbroker."

He visited the shells of cities, orphanages, and a destroyed mosque. The buildings started to fade into one another, and he needed Beba's help in keeping them straight.

Upon returning to his government's seat, he testified before a special commission for the former Yugoslavia.

"Frankly, gentlemen, they're all guilty as sin," he said, waving his arm in a wide circle. "They can't help it. It comes from a Byzantine nature."

He wasn't entirely clear on this perspective, historically speaking, but it seemed appropriate. Beba's eyes had a certain Eastern slant, and her nature was nothing if not shrewd.

"Yes, yes," someone on the committee said. "But, really, it's the thirty-ninth cease-fire violation."

"A terrible tragedy," he had responded, pressing his palms together in a cathedral and leaning his chin on the spire.

"I think it's time to discuss sanctions, lifting the arms embargo so that we level the playing field . . ." someone else chimed in. "It's most unjust to the Croatians and the Moslems."

He snapped to attention. "Good God, are you joking?" It had been his experience that the Croatians were politically inept and the Moslems were horrible whiners. At least with the Serbs, you knew what you got.

He managed to convince them that the war could not last forever. "Let it play out to its inevitable conclusion," he told them. "It's a universal law. Only one side can win."

But then the siege of Sarajevo started, and really the Serbs were becoming impossible. No sooner would they agree to halt shelling civilian sections of the city than they would unleash a firestorm on the maternity ward at the hospital. He had even gone to Pale in Republika Srpska for some shuttle diplomacy.

"Enough," he had told them. "You're making me look like an ass."

And they demurred, pushing a glass of something pale and fiery at him.

"My brother's orchard," the older man at his elbow said. He recognized the well-known, if not respected, philosopher who painted political murals in his spare time. The man had somehow negotiated to show his art abroad, though naturally such things were never explicitly stated in documents governing cease-fires or prisoner exchanges. His psychological theories were also well-known, especially the one concerning shepherds and their lambs, which he had shared at some prior point, with Beba interpreting and waving her arms demonstratively. It ran along the lines of THE LAMB LOVES THE SHEPHERD EVEN WHILE IT KNOWS THAT SLAUGHTER IS INEVITABLE.

At the time, the peacebroker had considered the man an imbecile. Later, he had changed his opinion. "Narcissist," he wrote finally in his diary.

In Pale, he took the *šljivovica* into his mouth and let it burn a path all the way down.

"My brother's orchard," the philosopher repeated. "On the hills outside Sarajevo." He had looked pensively at his own glass before draining it. "Beautiful country. Pretty girls. Fine winter sports."

The Serbs shelled a crowd of people waiting for humanitarian food rations dispersed from a truck. A shell had struck the truck bed and the pile of cans, and the metal had turned to shrapnel. Dozens died, dozens more were injured, and pieces of flesh littered the road.

A journalist had caught the whole thing on videotape, and by dinnertime the West had enough grisly pictures of death and destruction on their television sets to cause a swell of protest. The whole thing threatened to be a public relations mess.

At the beginning of the war, the peacebroker had attempted to make Sarajevo a journalist-free zone. He had been overruled on that point, and felt vindicated now. "Really," he said in a telephone conversation with his wife. "Maybe they'll listen to me next time."

Sarajevo's embattled authorities protested that the Serbs, who had been shelling and sniping the city, were responsible.

The Serbs denied it, their spokeswoman insisting that the city had shelled itself. "When," she beseeched the television camera, "will this madness end?"

He was quickly informed that the UN would be investigating. They had already dispatched a team of experts to the site, where they were busy measuring the dimensions of the crater, angle of impact, and strength of charge.

"Inconclusive," they said finally, shaking their heads. "It could have come from anywhere. Ruling out the possibility of self-immolation would be unwise at this juncture." The truck and several incidental bystanders had broken the shell's fall, and little could be definitively learned from the resulting crater.

He had been relieved. One could always count on the UN in this type of situation.

There were other troubling incidents. Peacekeepers accompanying a member of the Bosnian government opened the door to the APC in which they were traveling when armed Serbs would not let them pass. The gunmen killed the Bosnian on the spot, and the peacekeepers were said to be suffering post-traumatic stress disorder as a result.

The peacebroker felt a degree of unanticipated and fatherly protectiveness toward the peacekeepers. Like him, they had been through an awful lot. He gave, visibly and generously, to a psychosocial charity which funded centers encouraging peacekeepers to finger-paint and discuss their experiences through the medium of puppet theater.

There was plenty to act out, between incidents in which they were forced to hand over their pants to drunk and laughing militia and the pitiable lack of respect for their mission in the region. The fall of the Srebrenica safe haven had been a particular blow, with words such as "impotent," "cowardly," and "idiotic" bandied about in the press.

As for Kosovo, the less said the better.

Then the Americans bombed Serb positions and Belgrade itself. Beba had proudly worn a paper target on her bosom.

He had been recalled in advance of the bombings, and evacuated himself and Beba to the George V Hotel in Paris. She cut a handsome figure in the lobby, and people's eyes were repeatedly drawn to the defiant target. She had even gathered a circle of irate intellectuals around her. They were spoiling for a fight and met daily in an impromptu salon where Beba held court through a haze of cigarette smoke. They had managed several letters of protest in the press, and a famous performance artist in America sent word that she was planning a piece in solidarity with them. It would consist of a pyrotechnics display in which she dressed like a bomb and screeched "Imperialists!" at the audience. Beba planned to go to New York for the premiere.

Meanwhile, her Paris coterie hung on her every word. "Really," she told them, "we are a peaceful people." And he had winced again at her unfortunate pronunciation. "Persecuted since time began . . ."

But on the fifth day in the George V, Beba left him for an artist who created enormous phallic sculptures out of wet toilet paper. "You do not understand me," she told him accusingly. "You do not understand my Balkan soul."

And he had returned home to a university job and the remnants of his life. He had years of diplomatic service under his belt and frequently used his own experiences to illustrate his points. He rather liked teaching, all the fresh-faced students hanging on his every word. And he waited, quite patiently, for the next conflagration when he would again be called upon to provide his services. He practiced saying words like "internecine" and "quagmire" in the mirror.

He even had plans to write a book, a travelogue/war chronicle with character studies of the major players, maybe the hint of a love story.

And in the end he returned morosely to his wife, and to his collection of mismatched bottles. Sometimes, long after he had finished their contents, he would uncap them and smell their aromatic residue, the memory of fire.

Remains

THE SKY ABOVE THE TREES was black. But lying on the ground, he could see that the black was filled with blood-colored splinters of glass. Flecks of that sharp rain had already peppered his forehead, and a slow ooze hung above his brow before sliding down into his eyes and across his cheeks. Flipping onto his stomach, he blinked wildly and shook his head from side to side like a horse, trying to throw the muck from his face. He braced himself against the ground with his hands.

There were voices calling through the woods, and he strained to hear what they were saying. But the words were warbled rivers of noise and he put his forehead to the ground, trying to stem the flow and imagining the earth a giant, cold bandage. In fact, he could no longer be certain if they were voices, or blackbirds calling to each other from the branches of the trees.

When he sat up, he looked straight ahead. He knew that to his left lay a headless man. One quarter of the body was gone and the remainder was leaking into the cold ground.

Ten minutes before, he had risked using his lighter trying to identify it. The dim light still made it difficult to see and the bushes threw grotesque shadows across the ground. Though the blood had blackened everything, he had been able to make out two legs and an arm. At first he thought it was because of the shadows that he could not see the man's head, but then he raised the lighter higher.

It could have been anyone. It could have been his own body that he looked at, and for a startled moment he considered the possibility that his head had rolled neatly to one side and taken on a life of its own, and that he was viewing himself from that unlikely vantage. But the man in the weeds had been slighter than him, with his large frame, and the pain in his own body was sharp and real.

He heard a scrabbling sound to his left, but he could not bring himself to look that way again. He could imagine that the strange, three-pronged creature was rising, rustling the grass in which it had been lying. It would wrap its good arm around a tree, ascending to the top to survey the scene below, rocking against the sky, against the wind.

The voices were coming closer all the time. He could hear some in the distance and others so near they seemed to be right beside him. He leaned over again and buried his cheek in the dirt. *Hail Mary, full of grace*, he told the ground.

His wife, Nina, stood behind his eyes. In the kitchen, she looked out at the garden as she washed the supper plates. Another Nina was standing by the bedroom window holding the baby. Many Ninas, as if she were in a hall of mirrors.

He could hear the creature's ragged breathing as it worked its way slowly upward, and the footsteps as they came closer. His father's footsteps had been just that slow and measured. They had walked up and down the old barn, looking for him as he hid himself behind grimy hands.

"Where are you, Miš?" the voices were calling. "Where are you, Cigo?"

Cigo. Gypsy. That was the nickname they had given him because of his olive skin and black hair. *Joško*, he told the ground, his mouth in a grimace. *My name is Joško.*

There was a shuffling to the left and the right. They would converge on the spot where he lay, black night running like tar down his face. It was beginning to join him to the dirt. They would not be able to pry him loose from the ground when they found him. He would be like a tree that is uprooted only after considerable force, dragging away the earth still clinging to its roots.

"I see something!" It was a voice he recognized.

Silence.

He could feel them come upon the fallen creature. He could sense their surprise and shock as they shone the flashlight beam, and then someone began to cry.

They were carrying him beneath a canopy of pines, beneath the raining glass. He could hear it exploding in the air above them and falling in high-pitched whines onto the cover of trees. The pieces fell around them like a rainstorm in the woods.

The people transporting him suddenly lurched. The hands clasping his arms and feet almost lost their grip.

"Jesus!" said the voice nearest his ear. "Careful."

He began to talk, insistent and unintelligible syllables, and they stopped and placed him carefully on the ground. He could smell pine needles underneath him.

"Is he coming to?" asked another voice tentatively.

He was battling his way past the glass and stars to where the men were gathered in a semicircle around him.

"Where's Miš? Where's the boy?" His voice was dry and alien, but he was buoyed for a moment by its sound.

The men looked uneasily from one to another.

"Where?" he insisted, his voice cracking.

"He's dead, Cigo."

He tried to lift his head to look toward the voice but the effort was too much. The trees were going to fall down on him. The headless man was swinging among them like Tarzan, bending the boughs so violently that he nearly touched the ground.

When he finally regained consciousness, they had already removed one of his legs. Before a nurse could be summoned, he looked at the hospital linen that touched the bed where his leg should have been. Lifting the sheet to look at the bandaged stump, he began to cry.

There were other amputees in the room. The man nearest the window had a bandaged face and hands. The burns that kept him whimpering through the night had also blinded him.

"Go figure," said the man in the next bed, in one of the rare moments when they were both conscious. "They gave the bed with the view to the blind guy."

"Fuck you," came the response from the opposite end of the room.

The faces in the room changed constantly.

Sometimes, when the men in his unit were off the front line, they would come into the hospital room and visit him. They came one at a time, bringing him cigarettes and sitting on a metal folding chair next to his bed, their camouflage-covered legs stretched out in front of them. They would ask him if he remembered the ambulance or the medical station in Slavonski Brod, or the tall red-haired nurse who had bent over his shaking body and grasped his hand in hers.

"She was a looker. It's a shame you don't remember." They would grin uncomfortably as he lay there watching their intact bodies, covertly. Two feet, two legs, two arms, he counted out to himself each time.

But they were nervous and eager to leave, and Joško remembered that he too had once sat in a metal folding chair in that same hospital, but the man in the bed had not even been aware of him. Joško had shifted uncomfortably in the chair, leaving after only a few minutes, and the man died later that night. Joško had not thought of him since.

His commanding officer came as well, and they sat in strained silence. "It's not your fault," the older man said, finally. He had a square head and tough eyes.

"You told me to watch him." But he realized his voice lacked

all inflection. Its flatness startled him, but the man sitting next to
him did not seem to notice.

"I told you to show him how to do things the way you did
them. A shell hit him, for Christ's sake."

They sat in uncomfortable silence until Joško closed his eyes
and made the man in the chair disappear.

The men in the unit had nicknamed the boy Miš. Mouse. He
had not had any next of kin and they had brought his possessions
to Joško. A plastic bag beside the bed contained a razor, an identification card, and a snapped plastic rosary, its white string stained
a rust color. *Blood and dirt*, Joško had thought to himself when he
examined it. *Nothing but blood and dirt*.

"He was too young, anyway. He shouldn't have been there."
The seated man removed a handkerchief and wiped his forehead.
"How old do you think he was?"

But Joško pretended to be asleep.

Nina had started talking to him while they were dragging him
through the woods and fields to the ambulance. In the beginning,
her voice was just one voice in the chaos. Somewhere in the hospital it had become distinct, like a strand of hair which had lifted
away from thousands of others.

"Joško," she was saying to him. "Joško, wake up."

His eyes fluttered and he fought his way back, but when he
opened his eyes the folding chair was empty.

The man in the next bed was looking at him. "Your wife was
here. She went to ask the nurse something."

He turned toward the door, focusing all his concentration on
it. He listened for voices on the other side, footfalls that would an-

nounce her approach. He heard two voices, and again her voice separated from the other, becoming suddenly clear. There was a silence, and then he heard her push her weight against the door.

He watched her enter, but the features of her face never softened with recognition. Her hesitation made something in him curl and die.

"Joško?" She mouthed his name, her eyes huge. She looked just as he had remembered her.

He took the bedsheet in his shaking hands and uncovered himself. *There,* he thought, *look at what I've become.*

But she did not lower her eyes.

"Do you see?" he asked her roughly. The room fell silent.

"I see, Joško." The other men in the room were watching, but she walked across the room and climbed gingerly into the bed beside him. When she pulled the sheet over them both, it settled with a white whisper on her hair.

At home in Osijek he slept for weeks. Time passed uncertainly. The baby cried and he swam toward the surface for breath, only to turn and dive back under again.

Nina's voice came into his sleep as she talked on the phone. Snatches of conversation floated into him and sometimes he could hear her crying. Then, suddenly, she would materialize in front of him, opening the curtains to let in a little light. He hated the room's stale air, but he would glower at her until she retreated to other parts of the house.

Then the nightmares started. He would toss and turn, chasing pictures of Miš gushing like a river into the ground. The ground had been thirsty, it had sucked him up almost immediately.

"Joško!" The kid was calling in a muffled voice. "Joško, I'm here." Miš had been the only one in the unit who called him by his given name and not his nickname. He would turn around to see him, but it was always the same disfigured creature. The voice was coming from the chest cavity.

He would wake up whimpering, rise unsteadily, grasping his crutches, and watch his daughter sleep, Nina breathing softly in the bed behind him. He wondered what had become of his own leg, imagining its decomposition in the woods. *Or had they burned it?*

His pension was barely enough to buy food and diapers. The factory where he had worked before the war was closed, but he would not have been able to return there anyway.

The leg gave him considerable pain, and he hobbled about angrily on his crutches.

In bed one night he tried to embrace Nina but she shrank from him. "Your leg," she protested feebly.

"I don't fuck with my leg," he told her bitterly.

The words made her flinch, and the two of them lay there silently for several moments.

His hand wandered to her hair and she raised her own hand to grasp it. *I'm sorry, Nina*, he thought as she buried her face in his arm. *My life is nothing. I won't ever push our daughter's stroller, and I won't climb stairs. I'll never dance with you again.*

"I'm never going to be able to work," he told her the next day in the kitchen, his voice sounding final. He struck the stump. "Face it, this makes me worthless."

She was angry with him. "You think your worth is tied up in a leg, Joško?" she asked him quietly.

"It would have been better if I had died," he told her, throwing his crutches so that they crashed against the wall, chipping the paint. He watched the colors of fury collide in his wife's face and looked satisfied.

She stooped and picked up the crutches, holding them for a moment in her hands. "I ought to hit you in the head with these," she told him. Instead she balanced them once more against the table and turned from him to start dinner.

She began waking him from dreams with her hands and breasts. She leaned forward to cover his neck with her kisses and he swam out of fear into consciousness, her body arcing whitely above him in the dark. The bandages were gone, the scars where his skin closed over the stump were red and angry, but she kissed him even there.

In the morning he was never sure if he had dreamed that part.

The painkillers the doctor had prescribed for him were often not available at the city's pharmacies. Nina would wait in first one line and then another, only to be told that there was no medicine left.

"My husband is an invalid," she would tell the girl standing behind the counter.

"Lady, blame the Serbs, not me. The war has screwed up all of our supplies." This was the standard reply.

Without telling Joško, she answered an advertisement at a humanitarian agency that had just opened an office in town.

"Can you type?" they asked through an interpreter. "Speak any English?"

She shook her head and looked at the hands folded in her lap.

They had looked hesitantly at each other and then said, "We're also looking for a cleaning woman."

When she told Joško that night, his eyes bulged in their sockets. "Absolutely not."

She was feeding the baby and didn't look up. "It pays seven hundred German marks a month, Joško."

He rose, upsetting the chair as he retrieved his crutches. She could hear him hobbling away from her, into their bedroom. She knew what he was doing, and waited until she heard an empty bottle shatter against the wall.

The baby looked at her with a surprised expression, her mouth a perfect O as if she were deciding whether to cry.

"I won't if you won't," her mother told her softly, running a wet washcloth over her chin to wipe away the food which had dribbled there.

In the morning he would apologize, she knew. He would lower his face into his hands and tell her he was sorry. She sighed. She would wait a little longer, until she knew he was asleep, and then she would go in and clean up.

He had told her that Miš was from a village near Vukovar and his family had died in the first days of the war. They had gone up in smoke in their burning house while men waited in the front yard with machine guns ready to shoot anyone who tried to leave. Miš had been hiding in the field alongside the house. He had heard the screams and the rounds from the guns.

All the men in the unit had known this.

"Are you crazy?" they had asked him when he volunteered for the army. "You don't have to go."

"No?" he asked, his eyes flashing. "Where should I go then? Home?"

"You're too young," they had told him flatly.

"I'm eighteen," he had lied.

"Prove it."

He had smiled bitterly. "Get me back to my village and I'll show you my birth certificate."

He fought alongside the other men in the unit. He was a wiry kid with wheat-colored hair and a baby's complexion. His brown eyes could stare like twin bores, there was not a bit of light in them. Joško had never seen eyes like that.

"You shouldn't be here," Joško had told him once gruffly. "Don't you think you were saved for a reason? What would your parents say if they knew you were here?"

"They'd be proud," Miš had told him, chin jutting defiantly.

"Stick by me," he would tell Miš whenever shooting started.

Joško knew that Miš had been haunting him because of those words.

Miš tended to sit upright, the light-colored hair shining out of whatever landscape they were in. "Keep your head down," Joško had warned him on more than one occasion, planting his hand between the small shoulder blades and pushing him roughly into the ground.

Sometimes when she slept, Nina would be awakened by her husband's hand in the middle of her back, pinning her to the mattress.

"Stay down," he would whisper to her. "For God's sake, stay down."

Each morning at the bottom of their street, Nina would look left and right, standing on the curb. To the right was the center of town, and on the left lay miles of road and flat winter fields. She imagined walking through them, her footsteps increasing in speed until she was running. With her nose buried in her scarf, she inhaled the smell of wet wool and imagined the sound her boots would make crunching through the snow, beating the frozen ground like a drum.

When dawn started to send its threads through the sky, Joško would watch her through the kitchen window. Sometimes Nina waited until her hair was matted with snow before turning onto the road to town.

Afterdamp

Ja tebi pjevam jer si ti sloboda . . .
I sing to you, because you are freedom . . .
—JANKO POLIĆ KAMOV

IN THE AIRLESS BOTTOM of Mine Four he is remembering wind. The memory starts as a shiver. Lifting the pick over his head, he lets himself fall with it, the force of metal on stone creating an impact that rings in his bones and teeth. As the rock fractures, he imagines the wind on the back of his neck, underneath his helmet, like cool fingers.

Here in the shaft the air is always the same. It never varies, regardless of whether steam is rising in waves from the West Virginia ground outside or whether that same ground is hidden, frozen fast under a brittle crust of snow. Walking and crawling into the stomach of the mine each morning, he enters another country, a dead space where seasons do not exist. It is always uniformly cool in the mine, and damp. It is always uniformly still.

Performing his minute surgery on the hill's interior, he remembers how the gales had risen over the sea, pouring water onto the deck of their ship five years before. The ship lurched from side to side, like the violent rocking of a giant cradle. He remembers how the air filled with groans and the sour smells of people crowded into the hold.

His father lay beside him on the bunk, telling him stories about long-dead sailors who tied themselves to the rigging and masts to prevent being washed overboard in storms. He never stopped to ponder where his father, who had never seen the sea before that trip, acquired his information. He listened to still other stories of sailors who had trussed themselves to keep from jumping into the sea in search of mysterious, beautiful voices that called from the waves.

"Mermaids?" he had asked his father with a weak grin, his stomach pitching with the ship.

"Songs no man has lived to describe," his father insisted.

Abovedeck the air had been black with wind.

He stops himself at this thought. They had rarely been allowed abovedeck, so this is an imagined memory, and he shakes himself angrily in the stillness of the mine. Men on either side of him are hammering at the tunnel walls, creating a strange symphony of noise, but the still air produces a cool sweat beneath his helmet. He is unable for several moments to locate a memory of strong wind that is not borrowed from stories or myths, as if the world outside the mine were something that existed solely inside a children's tale, filtered underground from one dust-covered man to the next until reaching the very center of the hill where he is working, mutely swinging the pick and scrabbling through the black wall.

It is just as he begins to panic that something comes to him, so fragile that he stands completely still in order to receive it. *The wind was always running around Blidinje Lake.* He is pleased with himself and smiles, bending to consider the coal he has knocked loose and which covers the toes of his boots. There was always wind there, in the grasslands by the lake. It ran from the mountains and smelled of water and rock. Gentler in summer, it sent a soft yellow grit through the air. He would lie in the field behind the house, watching the falcons hunt in that amber wind. They lost momentum suddenly, hovering in place as if the wind had vanished. Treading wind like water, they studied the ground below before screaming and diving at lightning speed to grab a startled field mouse or mole.

In winter the lake would freeze and the fields were covered with a blinding snow.

"It's because we're close to the sky," his mother would tell him in the morning, dressing him in patched woolens and shoes that were too big. "We're closer than anybody to the sun."

When he crossed the fields, where the winter wind blew with biting fury, his fingers stopped bending and his face was left with reddened welts which cracked and bled in the evening by lamplight.

And at night, the stars shone out of a sky as black as the mine. Like a giant mourning cloth in which a thousand brilliant holes were punched, through whose peppered surface the wind walked freely.

He remembers this, picking up a piece of coal and removing his glove to test its oily blackness with his nail.

"My wife says you're to come eat your meal with us tonight, Matthew." The man has been working all morning just behind him in Mine Four.

He can find nothing to say. He remembers that the man's name is Joseph and that he and his family attend mass at St. Jude's. He thinks that one of the man's daughters is among the black-eyed girls who weave daisies into chains and crown themselves at church picnics.

"There'll be fish tonight."

He had forgotten that it is Friday. The days spin by one another quickly, piling up in grim lines.

The older man seems to be waiting for him to say something, and he looks at his feet awkwardly. Most men on the line keep their distance from him, as if he were a skittish animal that required careful handling. "Thank you," he manages to say.

In their first week underground he and his father had seen one of the mules go crazy. The mule had been dragging a coal wagon up to the surface from a narrower mine when the ceiling collapsed neatly on top of the wagon, crushing the thirteen-year-old driver but missing the mule, who stood twitching but quiet. Some flecks of razor-sharp coal had pierced his hide, and thick red drops fell on the dusty floor, but the animal was remarkably unscathed. When the men moved to cut him loose, however, the mule's eyes began to roll wildly. Once free, the mule bucked and jumped, throwing his body against the jagged sides of the mine, smashing his hooves and the bones of his legs. He rammed his head against the rock until blood matted his skin and soaked the rope and leather still muzzling him.

And he collapsed onto his knees like a fallen Goliath, panting on the ground until the men moved in and the foreman was summoned to place a bullet in his head.

It took them hours to remove the carcass from the mine. The mule had not picked a convenient place to die and they were a good distance from the entrance. It was only once they had dragged him aside, dumping him unceremoniously outside the mine's entrance, that they started to clear the fall-in, reaching the men caged on the other side.

Matthew remembers one thing with absolute certainty. As the foreman closed in, the dying mule's eyes suddenly shed their crazed light. When the man knelt behind him and placed the gun against his skin, the animal closed his eyes. And Matthew was sure that he was smiling.

They leave the mine at night, beneath a low and heavy sky. Joseph's house is not far from his own bunkhouse, although the mine company has tried to segregate the mining families from the immigrant workers, who are housed all together. They pass the dark windows of the company store in silence. Joseph's eldest, Sam, works in the mine at the crusher, and father and son discuss the upcoming baseball game against the Methodist team.

As they near the porch, Matthew sees that the house has a layout similar to that of the bunkhouse in which he sleeps. The company owns them all, identical wooden frames scattered across the entire hill. The hill itself is covered with dust and debris spat from the mine, but there is a strict line of demarcation at the entrance to

Joseph's house, where the women have swept the floor clean. For some reason, he is suddenly saddened by this sign of domesticity.

Joseph's wife is cooking, the oldest daughter helping her in a stained apron. When she sees Matthew standing on the porch, she pushes her hair nervously from her eyes. She is indeed one of the flower weavers, and he nods at her.

"Going around back to wash up," Joseph calls in to his wife, leading Matthew to the back of the house where soap and thread-bare towels have been set out for them next to tubs of water.

Matthew sheds his jacket and shirt, and starts washing the greasy dust from his hands and face. His clothing keeps the rest of him relatively clean. He pours water over his head, scrubbing the dullness from his jet-black hair. He cannot stand the feel of the sharp bits against his scalp. Joseph hands him a fresh, well-worn shirt which he slips on.

"Never can seem to get it all out." Joseph is looking mournfully at his nails, which are still black in the corners. "My wife has fits. When I get up in the mornings, there are black marks all over the bed."

Matthew had once been told that coal was actually dead matter, a million plants that had rotted and hardened underground. Sometimes after the worst mine disasters, it is too dangerous to reach the bodies and they are left, sealed underground. Looking at his own nails, dirt lodged in the white crescents, he wonders if those bodies will also turn into the hard black stuff.

"How old are you, Matthew?" Joseph's wife asks, feeding the baby. Five other children are seated around the table.

"Seventeen," he tells her. The little girl seated across from him is staring with wide eyes and he feels himself redden.

"A year older than our Louisa." She nods at her oldest daughter.

He bows his head and concentrates on finishing his meal.

She prods him. "And you're from Poland, then?"

He shakes his head. "Near from Poland," he tells her, although he does not actually know how far it is.

"I remember seeing you and your dad in church," she says absentmindedly, and then stops suddenly, looking away from him with an embarrassed expression.

Joseph's palm slaps the table, making the plates jump. "Leave the boy alone and let him finish his meal."

Matthew wants to tell him that it is fine to mention his father. Nobody has mentioned his father in days. It is as if he has ceased to exist in memory as well as in flesh. But he only bows his head and they finish the meal in silence.

After dinner they sit on the porch, listening to the sound of crickets. Matthew finds himself longing to leave and sits uncomfortably on the railing. The sound of Joseph's wife hurrying the younger children to bed makes him uneasy. It is an intimacy he shares with a rising tightness in his chest.

He stands abruptly. "Thank you for the meal," he tells Joseph, and steps off the porch.

"Come round on Sunday after mass," Joseph calls after him.

He does not respond. As soon as he is out of sight, he starts sprinting. His boots make the ground underfoot crunch and his eyes water in the wind he creates.

———

Before they even thought of leaving for America, a cousin who had returned from there had told them that they would have two choices. They could work either in the mills or in the mines. They came to West Virginia because that is where the other men they had traveled with were going. Some had brothers already working in the mines there, although within a year they had all moved on. Matthew and his father were the only ones from the original group who had stayed.

When they first arrived, he was too young to work legally in the mines.

"Age?" they asked his father, looking at Matthew.

"Sixteen," he told them, unsure of his English and a little shamefaced.

They raised their eyebrows and looked at Matthew.

"He's small for sixteen," they told his father.

He shrugged. "Small for age."

His father kept their wages hidden at the boardinghouse, using money only for their bare necessities.

At twelve, Matthew had understood that two wages would bring them back home more quickly. And they would not be separated, which was more important to him than anything else in this strange place.

He was not strong enough to lift the loads his father did, but because of his size he was able to wriggle into places that grown men could not. He could crawl blindly on his stomach, his small body pushing into the dark, and they met their quota every time. As he grew older, his size was compensated for by increasing strength.

But as he grew larger, his father also seemed to shrink. Soon

Matthew was doing the lion's share of the work, his father strug-
gling to keep up. They worked largely in silence, preferring to
speak only when they had quit the mine at the end of each day, and
then they were too tired to do more than exchange a handful of
words.

"You've turned into a solemn young man," his father told him
almost sadly one night. But then he brightened and told him, "Just
a little longer, and then we'll move on."

His father had started talking about moving to Pennsylvania
and the mills. But Matthew was interested only in returning to the
house beside the lake. When his father began talking of better con-
ditions and larger rations up north, Matthew felt his mouth draw
into a tight, straight line.

Better to starve in a familiar place, Matthew wanted to tell
him, but refrained.

One of the men in their bunkhouse had been there for fifteen
years. He spoke their dialect, having come from a village an hour
away from theirs, and often spoke with Matthew's father late into
the night, sitting on the porch of the house. The old man drank his
wages away and had not sent word to his family in years.

"They could be dead for all I know," he told Matthew's father,
who shook his head in disbelief.

"Old man . . ." he would respond, trailing off. He did not
know what to say.

The man had a cough that kept the others in the bunkhouse
miserable and awake. Black lung was far progressed in him, and
Matthew imagined a bed of decay in his chest, his lungs a bag con-
taining a heavy collection of coal dust.

The day they buried him, the priest said, "Dust to dust." And

Matthew imagined the man's carbonized skeleton, his dust-filled chest. When the ground broke through the rough wooden coffin and dissolved his skin, it would leave nothing but black coal behind.

Matthew had stopped meeting his father's eyes after that.

"A little longer," his father told him that night in the bunkhouse. "A little longer, and we'll leave."

The day of the accident, the foreman had sent him to work at the crusher. Matthew had been resentful. That job was usually reserved for younger boys, not someone seventeen years old. His father had gone with the other men into Mine Five, looking back once with a wave.

Around noon the siren screamed shrilly and he ran into the yard.

"Mine Five, Mine Five," someone was shouting in a frenzied voice, and he felt the blood drain from his face. He ran to the entrance, where a crowd had already started to gather.

"Afterdamp," someone whispered. It asphyxiated men, leaving them dead and contorted. The air suddenly seemed jaundiced to him and he put a hand to his mouth.

"We heard an explosion," he heard someone else in the crowd say.

The women had started to come to the mine entrance, some of them running down the hill with flushed faces. Still others came holding children's hands, babies tucked under arms.

"Mine Five," some said with relief. "It was just in Mine Five."

Men from other mines were locating their families in the

crowd, ushering them away from the scene and up the hills, into their houses where they banged the doors shut.

They were able to bring up some men from Mine Five, men whose faces were bleeding, or who were unconscious and on stretchers. The mine rescue workers came back a short time later, prompting cries from some people standing in the crowd. The man in front carried a caged canary. They turned back when the bird grew agitated from the poisoned air. The crowd parted to let them through and Matthew looked at the grim-faced man and the shuddering bird.

"My father?" he asked first one man and then the next as they exited the mine. He saw men from his bunk who walked by him blindly, blinking in the harsh light. They could not seem to focus on him until one of them ground to a halt in front of him, his chest rising and falling in violent movements. He looked at Matthew and shook his head. "He was working farther down from me."

There was no word that night, but he continued to stand outside the mine entrance into the next morning. By the end of the second day, they had prepared a list of ninety-six names. As they were read aloud, weeping broke out in the crowd. Women were led away by neighbors. He saw one woman sink to all fours on the ground, muddying her dress, pressing her forehead against the hill, as if in this position she could come closer to those who were belowground.

Later, they said that the men had been found in pairs, fathers and sons embracing in the bitter-tasting dark.

When his own father's name was read out, he did not recognize it.

It was surprising how many people from their region had made it to West Virginia. They formed an entire colony of men, attending mass at St. Jude's, filling the bunks of the houses alongside Italians, Poles, and Greeks. The air was thick with fathers and sons and brothers whispering about home, plotting their return in a handful of different languages.

My youngest will be about five now.

The wolves come close to the cisterns this year. They get bolder every year.

No one can cook like my wife.

No one has eyes like my wife.

Or a mouth so sweet, or arms so welcoming.

On paydays some of the men would get drunk, sitting arm in arm on the front steps of the bunkhouse, singing. The Greeks would clap as they sang. When asked, the Italians would say that they were singing about the sea. The songs circled each other, getting so enmeshed that the words no longer sounded normal without the accompaniment of foreign words and faces.

Some men lived there alone, without kin. They were the quietest. When they died, their countrymen might come and stand graveside, turning their beaten hats around and around in chapped hands. The Poles and Italians were buried at St. Jude's with rough wooden crosses. Sometimes after large accidents they were buried in groups, the rectangles of empty graves dug side by side. But they were still buried alone, unknown and unmourned, the other men frequently splitting up the few possessions left in the bunkhouse.

Their true names forgotten, obscured under years of coal dust,

they were entered into the register under American-sounding equi-
valents. Frequently no one could remember them being called
anything else. Just as he is now Matthew, and has to struggle for a
memory of his other, earlier self. For a memory of home, and of
wind. It is still a shock to him to realize that he has become one of
these men.

On his father's cross he carved the name, unsure even of its
exact spelling. He gouged out the grains of wood and left jagged
marks. He had cut his hands, and rubbed them across the rough
surface, bleeding through the letters.

"No use doing that, boy," they had told him. "The rain and
snow will rot his name right off before the year is out."

But he did it nonetheless, satisfied with his work. And he will
continue to recarve it at the end of each winter, for as long as he is
here.

He balked at sending word to his mother the last time he sent
money home, through some lucky emissary glad to be leaving this
place at last. She cannot read and he can barely write. "Tell her we
will soon be home," he tells the man.

In early morning, as the men in the bunkhouse are waking in
the half-light and rising to their feet with moans and dry coughs,
the air above his head is a weighty cloud. But the dreams fade
quickly from the air, the fields around the lake, the wind, and the
falcons dropping to the floor.

This Fertile Ground

WHEN WE WERE CHILDREN, our mother told us that no matter where the wind carried us, we were hard seeds. And that even if we were carried across oceans and mountains, inside us, hidden in our tough walls, lived the memory of who we were and where we came from. I remember how she opened a summer peach with her knife to show us. The rough exterior of the seed was blood red. I remember her words as I climb the ladder into the coolness of my fruit trees and place my hand on the bark. If I put my ear to the tree, I can hear its heart beating. I can hear it drinking the strands of water that thread through this ground in the springtime. If I shake the tree so that the boughs sway back and forth, I can hear the starchy hearts of all those seeds, jumping like smooth wooden pebbles in a thousand baby rattles. Survival is our goal, I tell the seeds.

The wind never carried me very far. For better or worse, God gave me an entire life in my hills. The house I live in is the house my father built. The one where, teeth cutting into cloth, I pushed my children into the world. Three who did not survive are buried in the graveyard. There are flowers in the tough soil of my garden that I have coaxed out. I put them on the tiny graves of my unforgotten ones. My brief children. My parents. My brother. It was always harder when they died away from us and there was no grave to watch over.

Now, they are still beyond me, but not for very long. In some moments, I catch myself remembering the girl, Marija, remembering how I had looked at old women, dressed in black with their clacking rosary beads and bright eyes. How they had watched us, just as I now unconsciously watch teenage girls in the village. Those women have gone; they are in that cemetery over there on the hill. Their ranks thinned and then were filled out again by my sisters and me, and by the friends with whom I spoke of love and babies, on hot days beside shaded creeks. Not all of us survived those darkest years, but those of us who did have moved into those old women's places, into the worn wooden pews they occupied in the church. Sitting on the thresholds of our houses, we watch the roads that have taken generations of our men away to the cities, to Germany and beyond. But I prefer to watch the fields, sitting in my kitchen doorway.

I lean in to hear my granddaughter singing. She has bare feet, brown with dirt and sunshine. Her mother will scold both of us for that, but I can deny her nothing. She has been playing earnestly with a doll. Her brothers are all in school, but she is still too young and is the last of them to leave my *dvorište*, my yard. I hang on to her most fiercely. There is a vague stirring in my head and the wind catches at a memory as at the pages of a book. She is singing a song that I remember my children singing. I find that time means nothing to me anymore, and that I seem to exist in many different places. The sun has made my hands brown and the shadow of my house is lengthening. Soon it will cover me and I will move my chair into the last little piece of light by the wall, until it too is covered in shade. The winter has been a long one this year. It almost killed one of the apple trees, but we have nursed it back to life. So, I tell my granddaughter's bent head, we deserve a little sun.

Age fades memory. It is my eyes, Old Marija's eyes. The world has blurry edges, indistinct corners and objects which combine. That is why I have kept the photographs. In their yellowness, I am that young woman again. I am constructed of air and my children are eternally children. My brothers are alive. My brother Petar was the oldest. And then Mile. Mate and I were twins. I have not decided if it is punishment or reward when I open the box of photographs, when sleep descends and I dream of them.

It is always summer and we are always barefoot. In the years before the wars, our house was on a dirt road in the country, and not on the outskirts of town as it is now. There were fields on either side of us, whose color and smell are still the same today. Dark brown fields in spring, when the snowmelt made them wet, they were hot and dusty in summer, and the wind dressed you with their yellow grit.

Petar and Mile always ran ahead. They were sturdy boys who helped our father in the field. As often as not, they came home with ripped clothing and scrapes, but Mate had an altogether different constitution, slight and fair like our mother. He seemed resident of a different place. The schoolmaster lent him books that he never lent to the other children, which made them turn on him, pummeling and pushing him. In the beginning the older boys tested his sturdiness, but even though Mate was built of glass, it was a tough glass with thick walls. They would pick on him when our brothers were not around to stand up for us, and his nose was regularly bloodied. Until one day they pushed me so hard I fell and burst into tears. My hands were raw and muddy. I remember the expression on his face as if I had it in a picture, that moment of electricity before lightning strikes. And then Mate lowered his head like a bull and charged. In the end, we stood in the track watching the boys run away. The one who had pushed me was shrieking, holding his arm to his chest. It was bent at an odd angle, and every running step he took produced a new wail, so that he sounded like a siren running away from us. We looked at each other, listening to the *woo-woo-woo-woo* disappear. They left him alone after that.

In one dream we are running across the field to our house. Our mother is waiting with dinner. We are a train, cars moving in unison, our feet kicking up dust around us. We run a long time like that. When I wake up, I have the feeling that we are still running. As I, the old woman, prepare to open windows and make beds, the little girl is still running somewhere with her brothers.

I never dream of the later years, of the blackness that descended on us like a universe of locusts. Of all that famine and killing, when they tried to erase us. They removed our skin and our flesh. If it were up to them, they would not have left even our bones behind. The bodies in the rivers do not float into my dreams. My brother Petar does not come and wail under my window, his body rattling with a great weight of bullets. I am spared that particular cross.

Mate joined the priesthood. It was the natural course of events, and our mother was so proud. She had given three children to the world, but she had given Mate to God. He joined the Franciscan order. When the war began he was finishing at the seminary, but he did not see the end of the war. My twin would not be the teller of our histories as I had hoped. In those days the fruit trees shed their leaves as if they were crying. The sun did not shine. It burned us to black and incinerated our bones, so that we became walking ash.

They had come at night. They sneaked up to the church and slit his throat and the throats of the two other priests. When I heard of it, I could not stop picturing it. The look of surprise and sorrow. The way he sank to his knees and into the ground. This ground.

My eldest brother, Petar, died in a distant place. In Bleiburg, when they retreated all the way to Austria. The Partisans caught up with them there and shot him and his wife and infant son, along with thousands of others. It was never mentioned. Or it was said that they deserved it, that it was a settling of accounts. But by that reasoning, who would die because of Petar and our people? Mate would say, no one. Because killing does not bring balance. I put the white star-shaped flowers on Mate's grave. Petar has no grave, so I think of him when I am in the trees.

When the first reports of the Virgin appearing in Međugorje reached us, I was happy. And then the fear crept in. My husband, who had worked for almost our entire marriage in Germany, had just recently come back. He had broken four ribs and hurt his back in a building accident.

"I'm afraid," I told him suddenly.

He was chewing on his lip and looked at me impatiently. "Because of what?"

"Will they let it happen?" I asked tentatively. "Won't they try to stop it?"

He looked as if he might get angry, and then started to laugh. "If the Virgin Mary has decided to come, then I don't think they have anything to say about it." He was entertained by this thought and went off laughing to himself. "They can't throw *her* in jail."

We loaded assorted children and grandchildren into the car and joined the procession up the dusty track to Međugorje.

My mother, who was still alive then, believed it was the natural course of events. Of course she would appear to us, her children in Herzegovina. She was the only softness in our universe. The dark church on a scorching day, whose dark doors were pools of cool stone.

Her face, the most beautiful of faces. Flickering of candles, and the smell of years of incense. The stones worn by the feet of the people we have forgotten, just as we will be forgotten. Her blue robes, her sweet expression. Her son clasped to her chest, and her eyes fixed on the church's sky. The look on her face is one of patience and suffering, Mother of Sorrows. That is why we love her. Because there is no sorrow so great that she will not under-stand and intercede on our behalf. We were told not to give our children religion, that it would pollute their minds and stand in opposition to them joining the brotherhood of people. But we never wanted our children to join their brotherhood. They knew that and hated us for it. We would keep our hills, our customs, our religion. They were strangers to us.

I take the knife in my hands. I must be careful, because the knife is razor-sharp and my hands shudder as if they have a mind of their own. My granddaughter leans in to see, her bent head brushing my cheek, her eyes wide and serious. She is concentrating on the shiny blade, which is seeking the crevice of the peach pit. It makes a grinding sound and then, suddenly, slides in clean. One quick movement and the pit lies in two halves on my palm. I take the tip of the blade to show her the spongy white center of the seed. She lowers her face to it and sniffs. A smile breaks across her face. She tells me, "*Baka*, it smells like your trees."

The Daughter

THE FIRST NOTE SLID beneath her door as small and perfect as a miniature ray gliding at the bottom of the sea. She stared at the neatly folded square on the floor of her room. She did not hear the sender's footsteps recede in the hallway outside and for a moment believed she heard the heartbeat of someone waiting on the other side.

It was evening, long after most students had wandered back from dinner at the university cafeteria, and she was suddenly conscious of every echo in the cinder-block dormitory. People paced back and forth above her, and somewhere on her own hall someone had turned on a radio.

From where she sat, she could see her name written in someone's even hand on the note. *Saša*. The penmanship was very masculine, she thought to herself, very spare. Someone who knew her and thought of her fondly, else he would have written Aleksandra and not its diminutive.

She rose but did not cross the room. Something made her want to prolong this moment. To keep the note bringer waiting in fraught anticipation.

Outside her window two people were in conversation, and she imagined them sitting together on the iron benches beneath the trees that graced the front of her building. The boy's voice was low and guttural. His female companion laughed softly. The sound made the hair on her own arms stand up in expectation.

When she could stand it no longer, she walked over to the door on tiptoe and opened it with a dramatic flourish, something comical on the tip of her tongue. *Have we met somewhere before?* Or, *Fancy meeting you here.*

But when she saw that the hallway was empty, her planned witticisms shriveled. The lightbulb outside her room had burned out and not yet been replaced. All the other lamps on the hallway were working and the sole patch of darkness was outside her own door. The hallway was still, and the only sign of movement was from an open window at one end, where a cord from gray decrepit blinds swayed in a breeze. It tapped against the sill, and she stood a moment listening to its steady rhythm. The dormitory seemed to have fallen silent when she stepped into the hallway, and the narrow corridor magnified the sound of the cord like a giant woodwind instrument.

She retreated into her room, closing the door behind her.

"What have we got here?" she asked the letter conspiratorially, holding it for a moment in both hands. She returned to the desk and looked at it under the lamp, noting the thickness of its nicely milled paper. It had a weight to it, not like that cheap, almost plastic-looking paper they sold by the ream in stationery stores around campus. She lifted it to her face and sniffed. Definitely a man, she thought, smiling. There was the faintest aroma of shaving cream or cologne. Something spicy, and fleeting. She imagined someone carrying it in his breast pocket.

Šerlok Holmz, she joked to herself.

She unfolded the paper slowly. Relationships started this way, and led to love, marriage, and honeymoons in elegant places such as Rome or Paris. Books were written on this subject.

She had never been outside Yugoslavia, not even for her senior class trip shortly after the war had started, when her father said it was an extravagance to go abroad at such a time. The trip was canceled anyway, because who wanted to go into the world when the world so obviously despised you?

The paper was porous. In her hands it felt like human skin, and she leaned forward with such yearning that she felt at once silly and vindicated.

The girl outside in the courtyard laughed again, louder this time, and the sound sent a shiver of anticipation down her own back. It was the sound of gentle teasing, the anthem of intimacy.

She opened the paper so that it lay flat upon her desk, her lamp making it glow like a shaving of white marble. Her heart stood still for a moment as she read.

Murderer's daughter.

She did not tell her father. With his temper, she could imagine the fuss he would make and the guards he would station outside her door. She did not tell her mother, whose voice sounded farther away with every phone call. On weekends when she went home, she neatly avoided all conversation about her social circle.

"Our Saša is a bookworm," her father teased. "No use for friends or boys when she's got organic chemistry."

She took his mockery good-naturedly, even grinned.

"Never you mind," her mother chimed in. "There's time enough for that."

"Besides," her father added, "I don't think I'd approve of the boys there. Who are their fathers? What have they done for Serbia?" He waved his hand dismissively. "The faggot sons of artists and intellectuals," he said, "avoiding the draft."

Such trips depressed her immensely. She knew the people her father considered suitable, and their ranks filled her with hard, cold dread. He had no interest in the people she enjoyed, and for that matter had little patience with university education. In his mind it was good for one reason only. Improvement of pedigree, and only for girls. Times being what they were, he had insisted, true men went into the business of war as soon as they were able.

It had not taken her long to see the reality of her situation at the university. Her father's reach extended even there. After her first examination, for which she had stayed up long hours studying and writing notes, the papers had been returned to her with only one notation. *A—excellent work*. At first she was exultant. The people to either side of her had groaned at their own results, and she had looked at their papers surreptitiously.

It was a shock when she realized that she had gotten the first question wrong. And the fourth. Still a well-written test, but perhaps not an A. She had been confused, but brushed it off, considering it nothing more than a stroke of luck.

"Saša, that's wonderful!" her mother had told her when she telephoned, then hesitated. "But why don't you sound happy?"

She had the same professor for several subjects, and on his next test she deliberately missed three questions. Again, he did not catch her errors. On the third test, she made sure that every other answer was wrong. And again she received the same result. *A—excellent work.*

She went to see her professor during his office hours. On the other side of the door, she could hear him talking on the telephone. His voice was muffled, but she could make out its lightness. She pushed open the door and nodded shyly. He was leaning back in his chair with his legs on the desk.

When he caught sight of her, he snapped to attention. "I'll call you back," he told the person on the other side, and hung up hurriedly, almost guiltily.

"I'm sorry to disturb you," she told him.

"No, it's nothing. Nothing!" He jumped to his feet and cleared books off another chair. "Please, sit. It was just my wife . . ." His chuckle had an edge to it.

She settled herself in the chair, holding the three tests on her lap. She could feel her face grow quite flushed, and when she began to speak there was a quiver in her voice. "I don't understand, Professor. I think you have made some errors in grading my tests . . ."

"Errors?" He looked surprised, reluctantly taking the papers she pressed into his hands. "I don't think so, dear."

"Yes," she insisted, sitting ramrod straight. "You see, I quite purposely wrote the third test poorly"—she indicated the last page—"but I got the same results."

"No, no," he said with a smile. "You're a very good student. One of my best." He rose abruptly. "You must excuse me, I have another lecture to teach in ten minutes."

She hesitated a moment before rising as well. He was shifting from foot to foot, but would not meet her eyes.

"I studied for that first test," she told him in a burst. "And it was good, but you never read it. What's the point, then, of my studying?"

"Please," he said apologetically, looking at his watch.

She almost stomped her foot in frustration. She could feel her eyes filling with tears and looked away so that he would not see. But before doing so, she noted that he had broken into a sweat, although the room was quite drafty and the radiator obviously broken. The perspiration hung on his upper lip in tiny beads.

She turned and stumbled from his office.

On the next test, and on every test thereafter, he marked two of her wrong answers. The writing was tiny, nearly contrite, but each time the result was the same. *A* and *excellent work*.

The second note was placed in her gym bag while she waited in line at the swimming pool. Although she was conscious of being jostled, she was intent on showing her student card and entering the building. When she went to change, however, she realized with a sinking heart that the bag was unzipped partway. She expected to find her wallet missing but instead found another piece of white paper. This time it was a black-and-white Internet printout, an article from a Western paper accompanied by a grainy photograph. She dropped heavily to the bench in her dimly lit changing cabin. *Your father is a murderer who does his job well.* The same now-familiar handwriting.

She examined the photo more closely. It showed a village in Bosnia burning in the background, smoke billowing into the sky. In the foreground was a pile of bodies. She did not bother to read the article but tore the page up, scattering the shreds on the wet floor. She watched as a puddle soaked one of the pieces, making the lettering thick and waterlogged. The edges blurred and the ink ran. It looked like blood from where she sat.

She was not unattractive, but she was shy. She was not unfriendly, but she was shunned. At night she closed the shades on her windows very tightly and drew the covers up over her head. She had been so sure the first note was a love note, and now she laughed and cried herself to sleep in a fit of self-loathing. She had thought it might be from one of the boys in her class, or the guy who worked the evening shift at the dormitory's reception desk downstairs. He had smiled at her several times as she passed and even greeted her once in the cafeteria.

She had asked him to have the light outside her door fixed. The next morning the bulb had been replaced. But when she returned that evening from her classes, it was missing. She had stared dumbly upward for a moment before unlocking her door with a pounding heart. But nothing in the room had changed, and nothing was amiss.

They came to replace the bulb several times more, but each

evening she would return to her dormitory to find the familiar sight of her doorway bathed in shadow. She learned to live with that little patch of darkness yawning outside her threshold and told no one.

Although it was unnecessary, she threw herself into her studies. She wanted to be a veterinarian and spent long hours in the research laboratory with the animals. She let silken-eared rabbits or tiny white mice out of their cages and stroked them in her lap.

She dreamed of one day owning her own apartment in Belgrade with a menagerie of animals. She would have cats and dogs, and a rabbit hutch on the balcony. She would be left alone with her animals and emerge only to visit her parents and get food.

One of the experiments the university lab was conducting had to do with the absorption rates of poisons. She hated it. The shuddering bodies were injected, variables were noted, and the animals were monitored every few minutes for the decreasing movement which preceded death.

She insisted on being in the lab for these experiments, and even held some of the animals in her hands as they died.

The experiment's monitors, other students, watched her strangely as she sat huddled on swivel chairs with her expiring charges.

One of them, a boy her age with brown eyes, brought her a cup of coffee one evening. "It is necessary," he told her gently. "Why do you make it harder on yourself than you must?"

Her head snapped up angrily at this kindness. But she softened under his concerned gaze. She took the coffee gratefully and drank. "Remorse," she told him.

Printouts of other articles were slid under her door or left in places where she would find them. Once, in the laboratory, she noticed that the rabbits' cages had been lined with them. There were pictures of emaciated men, their bones jutting from their skin like sticks, and of crying children. There were pictures of corpses and villages laid waste.

This time she read them. She moved from cage to cage, holding each animal, removing each sheet of paper and replacing it when she was done. *The New York Times. Corriere della Sera. Die Zeit. The Guardian. El País.* Even *Oslobođenje.* She understood most of the English, some of the German, and none of the French and Italian. But she saw that her father's name was everywhere.

At night the faces of those corpses from the newspaper photographs would come into her dreams. They would say nothing, but stood looking at her. During the days, she spied them around campus, in academic buildings, and in line at the cafeteria. They began attending some of her classes and swam in the lane next to hers at the pool. No matter how quickly or slowly she swam, if she looked over to her left or right, they would be keeping time with her, their limbs greenish in the chlorinated water.

She rarely went home, and when there she spent long hours shut away in her room. If she looked out onto the street, they clustered beneath one of the lamps. And she marveled at their defiance in the middle of strictly patrolled Dedinje.

"What is wrong with you?" her mother asked her. "You're so thin and pale."

Her father was rarely home. On one occasion when he was, she left some of the newspaper printouts on his desk.

"What is the meaning of this!?" he shouted at her. "How can you believe the things they write? I am your father, how can you not know me?"

She wanted desperately to believe him. "Then they are lies?" she asked hopefully, near tears. "The photographs are fabrications?"

He hesitated and her heart sank like lead. It made a hollow sound as it dove down, down past every other organ, down into the shiny parquet of their floor, where it buried itself completely. "Liar," she told him quietly.

He looked at her in shocked surprise. "How dare you question me?"

The animals were killed off one by one, including the control group, which, according to the laws of empiricism, could not be used in another experiment. A new shipment of rabbits and mice arrived, but she found that she had no interest in their twitching noses, or their unpolluted fur which still carried the scent of the outside and innocent world.

She stopped going to her classes and to the cafeteria. She stopped bathing and changing her clothes. More notes were pushed under her door, and she read each article carefully before refolding it and placing it atop one of the neat piles on her desk. The content had not changed, and her father's name was ubiquitous. But the handwritten message was new. *Justice*, each new piece of paper demanded.

Her mother grew frantic, ringing the reception desk and leaving messages for her to call home. These were also pushed under the door, and she made another, separate pile of them.

When she removed the razor blade from its package, she was quick in the incisions, as if at the dissecting table in her biology class. They were professional cuts, and she admired their bold strokes. She crawled into bed, the blood rushing quickly to make it a warm, moist cocoon.

It seemed to her as she walked out that she passed the bleeding bodies of other women, pushing the headless torsos of their men in wheelbarrows. It seemed that villages burned on each side of her, blocking out the sun and causing ash to fall in her eyes and on her hair.

Her father was nowhere to be found, but his work was everywhere.

Adiyo, Kerido

THERE WERE SONGS from Bosnia whose words Javier understood, despite the fact that he was Argentine. The songs were not in Bosnian, the Slavic and blunt-edged language that he associated with gaunt faces, cheekbones protruding like elbows, but in Spanish. It was a crazy Spanish with antiquated forms, Italian additions, and pronunciations that made him smile. He had heard these songs before. When he was a teenager, a group of Ladino singers had come through Buenos Aires on a South American tour, singing at the Jewish Community Center. They had been from Bosnia, Greece, and Turkey. From North Africa and Israel. And from Italy, like his own grandparents, who had reached Buenos Aires by ship in the 1930s. It was an epic journey, his grandmother had told Javier jovially on more than one occasion, resulting in claustrophobia, seasickness, and his father.

By the time Javier reached Sarajevo in 1996, most of the Ladinos had disappeared. Their community had been decimated in the Second World War, and most of those who had survived were evacuated at the beginning of the siege to Israel, and to points east and west. Their music remained behind, however, like a soft wind that blew in and out of Sarajevo's mutilated architecture and through her makeshift graveyards.

That summer, Javier was working on forensic excavations in a small town some distance from Sarajevo. He visited the capital on a rare day off. He had agreed to meet two friends who were journalists, but on condition that they refrain from asking questions about his work, and that they steer him to a place where he could have a decent meal. He had spent days in the field subsisting on thick, dry crackers from UN "Meals Ready to Eat," regarding with skepticism and distaste the powdered contents of envelopes which promised to convert themselves into "Pasta and sauce" or "Beef stew" upon addition of water. One of the friends, a Spaniard, had told him of a restaurant whose steaks were the best in the entire region, and Javier planned to join them there for dinner.

He arrived in Sarajevo earlier than expected and walked leisurely around Baščaršija, the old market section of the city, looking at the outdoor stands and merchandise that hung in front of the shops. The war had been over for a year, and pedestrians were able once again to stroll unhindered by shelling or sniper fire. He watched the couples walking together, some with small children in strollers. Old men in dusty black suits congregated in the street. From their gesticulations and disgusted expressions, he knew they were talking about politics, and he smiled inwardly at the universal language of their waving hands.

He wandered into one dark shop where piles of copper pots and silk scarves covered every surface. A dirty glass case contained filigree jewelry, and his eyes were drawn to a pair of intricate earrings. He was tempted to buy them for his girlfriend Alba, a lawyer in Buenos Aires.

Javier was summoning the storekeeper, a young man with a shock of black hair and white skin who was smoking behind the counter, when his gaze fell upon a pile of cassettes stacked haphazardly on top of the glass. He was struck for a moment by the incongruity of Spanish words.

Selecting one cassette, he turned it over and read *Adiyo, kerido.* "*Adiós, querido.*" He stiffened, realizing that he had spoken aloud.

"I play for you?" The young man asked in English, stepping from behind the counter. Not waiting for Javier to respond, he took the cassette, opened the unsealed cover, and slipped the tape into a dusty black radio behind the counter.

A woman's voice began, warbling slightly. *Kwando tu madre te pariyo, i te kito al mundo, korazon eya no te dio para amar segunda.*

The storekeeper looked at him expectantly. "It's Ladino. A song from Sarajevo's Jewish community."

Javier nodded absentmindedly, listening to the words. *When your mother bore you and brought you into the world, she gave you no heart to love another.*

He bought the cassette and the earrings. The music played on in his head as he thanked the man, tucking the purchases into his jacket pocket. It continued throughout the fine meal when the details of his work were temporarily forgotten as they discussed more general themes. Though he had spoken English fluently for years, his mother tongue was still a refuge into which he happily fled. But his friends began to tease him when, for the third time, he missed what they were saying.

"Love songs," he said cryptically and with a slight smile.

He listened to the cassette on the drive from the city back to the apartment he had rented on a hill above a town whose face was as scarred as that of every other town he had just passed through. When he got out of the car, the saline light of the Milky Way curved through the black night above his head, no streetlamps to pollute the darkness.

He had chosen forensic anthropology over other subjects, and his parents had not approved.

"For God's sake," his father had said, "of all things."

He could have been a businessman or a lawyer, or a doctor like his father. But there was something about bones that interested him. And there were the memories of Argentina's dirty war, when thousands of people, including his mother's younger brother Simón, had disappeared. *Los desaparecidos.* As if the air had eaten them whole.

Simón had been a lawyer and his favorite uncle. On a summer day in 1980, when Javier was sixteen years old, Simón failed to return home for dinner. His wife, Lucía, telephoned them in a panic, asking if they had seen him. His office was locked up neatly behind him, a man from the neighboring office had seen him leave, but they could not find anyone on the street who had witnessed his passage, somewhere between work and home, from being into nothing.

"Maybe he emigrated, señora," the police suggested, smiling.

Javier's family knew that he had been detained. He had secretly done pro bono work for unions, although he was hardly an activist.

"Your uncle was a thinker, a dreamer," Javier's mother had told him in tears. "And the world is filled with bastards who hate him for it."

With luck, Simón would be released after a few days or weeks, or maybe even months of incarceration. He would return gaunt and beaten, calling out in the middle of the night but reticent about his absence. That did happen in some cases, Javier's mother reminded everyone.

Simón never returned, though, and the family had inherited his absence like a disease. It tainted all the years that followed. There were constant reminders that he was gone: birthday parties, graduations, and other family celebrations. Every time the family crowded together for a photograph, Simón's face was missing. The absence tore through album after album, hovering in the blank space over their heads, throwing its phantom arms around their shoulders so that their smiles were something less than smiles. And the eyes turned toward the camera all contained the same question.

Javier knew the answer to it. In the late 1980s, excavation had started on sites around the city, and he had involved himself in the slow process of identification. He knew when he examined the bones in the forensic labs. He knew when he visited the burial sites—haphazard piles in garbage dumps, in fields outside the city.

"If you ever find your *tío* Simón," Lucía had told him, "you must tell me."

He had looked at his aunt in discomfort. "I will, *tía*."

"You mustn't keep it from me, you know. You must tell me right away."

He nodded. In all the years of performing the identifications, he had kept it in the back of his mind. He determined age and sex in the bones, approximated heights. He examined dentition, looking for the familiar gap in the front two teeth.

After graduating from university, he took a job with a forensic team that traveled around the world. They worked in Southeast Asia and Africa. He returned to Argentina and worked there, moving on to Guatemala and Chile. He had even helped identify victims from an airplane crash in the gray Atlantic waters off the Canadian coast.

He thought of himself as a solver of puzzles. The bones were pieces that, together, made a picture. From the picture, he was capable of divining answers.

Bosnia was different from what he had expected. He had continued his education at a European university and attended conferences in various European capitals, but he had never actually worked there, and certainly not on mass-grave sites.

The team had come to Bosnia after several months in Rwanda. The work had been exhausting and the African climate had drained them almost completely. Half of the team was sent home to recuperate.

Javier had already promised Alba he would be coming home for two weeks, and she had arranged to take time off from work.

"It's a lot to ask, we know," his office had told him over the phone, "but we really need you in the field by next week."

By the time he arrived, excavations had been under way for several weeks. They were excavating in a town still under Serb control inside Republika Srpska, and would then move on to sites in Federation Territory.

There had been considerable tampering at the first grave site, and they were afraid that their arrival would provide the impetus for more. Before hiring guards from abroad, they took turns watching the site. Javier had spent several uncomfortable nights in the bed of a truck parked on the road above the grave. Once excavated, the bodies were stacked floor to ceiling in a container and transported out of Republika Srpska to Federation Territory, where they were deposited outside a makeshift morgue and laboratory.

They hired locals to wash the clothing from the corpses. A group of sturdy youths and a man who looked around thirty, they were largely silent and watched the delivery of the first container from a careful distance. They spent the days over the wash buckets speaking among themselves. The older one, a man with opaque black eyes, spoke a little English, and it was to him that the international anthropologists and pathologists gave instructions.

When they had gone through the first container, a second was delivered on the bed of a huge truck. Javier stood outside, watching as they lowered it onto the concrete in front of the morgue.

"*Sramota.*"

He turned and saw that the worker with black eyes had come to stand behind him. The man was watching them unhook cables from around the container and set up the refrigeration system.

"Sorry?" Javier asked.

"Shame," said the man. "Those people wanted get out"—he held up a hand with splayed fingers—"four years ago. They could not. Only now." He looked at the container and Javier looked as well. "And now is too late."

The man turned on his heel, walking back into the morgue.

Javier continued to watch them inspecting all the machinery and gauges that prevented any further decomposition. As if the container were an incubator, sustaining the dead.

Sometimes he slipped the cassette into his radio and sat at the table drinking coffee in the morning. At night he slept, largely untroubled by the work he did during the day. The truth was that he was fascinated by the science of it, the intricacies of the puzzle.

It was the women who stood at the fence that disturbed him. They had started coming a month into the investigations. The team was trying to operate anonymously, but word spread quickly and the region was filled with people who had been displaced from areas still under occupation.

Initially they came singly or in small groups and looked into the yard where the washed clothing of the dead was hung to dry in the sun. They stood there wordlessly, scanning the sweaters and pants and shirts.

When one woman passed out from the heat, having walked, they learned, thirteen kilometers in order to see if there was any article of clothing that she recognized, their team leader had put her foot down.

"We can't have this. Pretty soon the entire town is going to be out there standing at the fence."

They attached blue plastic tarps to the fence, lashing them

through with white cord. When the wind blew, they looked like the sails of a strange, snaking ship.

But the women continued to come to the fence. They took turns peeking between the gaps in the tarps, trying to make out something familiar. Javier could see them watching him when he smoked in the shade of the wall outside the morgue. Eventually he would throw the cigarette down and turn back inside, feeling their eyes on his back.

Two weeks after his return from Sarajevo, he went into town to buy fruit from the marketplace. An older woman shopping at the same stall recognized him.

"I know you," she told him in accented English.

He looked at her closely, taking the oranges he had just purchased and depositing the loose change from the vendor in his pants pocket. Her hair was jet black, shot with silver. His first thought was that she looked like his *tía* Lucia, and his second that he needed to get far away from her.

"You are working at the morgue."

The man selling the fruit looked up, scanning his face as if seeing it for the first time.

Javier nodded, and turned away.

"No, wait!" The woman put a hand on his arm. "Please. May I offer you a coffee?" She nodded toward a series of refreshment stands set up on the far side of the marketplace.

"I don't think—" he started to say.

The woman smiled at him. "I saw you through the fence. You would not turn down an old woman, no?"

He shifted from foot to foot, the oranges like a burden in his hand.

When they were seated at a plastic table in the shade, he took out his cigarettes and offered her one.

She took it, grinning, and allowed him to light it for her. "You should not smoke," she said through the gray cloud she exhaled. "Is very bad for you."

He smiled in spite of himself.

She ordered coffee for them both. When the waiter arrived and placed the shallow white cups in front of them, she began speaking very softly.

"The bodies are from occupied territory, no? I think they're from my town."

They were under strict orders not to divulge information and he could feel his jaw tighten. "I'm sorry, I can't tell you that."

She went on as if she had not heard him. "They are, they are."

"How do you know?" he asked.

"My neighbor saw her husband's shirt through the fence."

He shook his head. "It's hard to see anything from twenty meters away."

"You don't understand. She made that shirt for him."

He looked at the coffee in the tiny cup. Bosnian coffee was cooked in the Turkish way, and boiled to a dark sludge that seemed to coat every organ of the body on its way through the digestive system. He raised it to his lips, and drank until the grains burned the back of his throat.

"It's hard to mistake such things."

"Perhaps." He lowered his cup. "You speak English very well."

"Yes." She smiled. "I was a teacher before the war. I studied literature at the university."

He nodded.

"Your English is not bad either," she added. "You are Spanish?"

"Argentine," he told her shortly. "What is it that you wanted to know?" he asked. She recoiled at the note of impatience which had crept into his voice and he regretted it immediately. But he could not open himself to the sorrows of people in every place, on every job.

She stubbed her cigarette out in the overflowing ashtray between them and he stared at the glowing end before it drowned, finally, in the pile of ash. "My son is missing."

He nodded. "I'm sorry, but it would be impossible for me to say—"

She put a finger to her lips, silencing him, and he felt his heart sink. He shouldn't have joined her.

"It will be easier to identify him than the others," she told him.

He raised his eyebrows.

"His right eye was made out of glass. Dark blue." She placed her cup back on its saucer and summoned the waiter. "There were problems during labor. Not enough oxygen, the doctors said . . ."

He shook his head, pulling out his wallet. "You're right, that would be something we would remember. No, not yet."

She put a hand over his, pushing the wallet away. "No," she said shortly. "I invited *you*." She handed some notes to the waiter and rose to her feet unsteadily.

He rose as well, standing awkwardly as she tucked her bag under her arm.

"Your oranges," she reminded him, pointing to the seat that had been beside his.

He bent to retrieve them, and rose to find her eyes on him, large and bright. *She is trying not to cry*, he told himself. *She is telling herself that she will wait to cry later.*

He felt his shoulders jerk slightly. "I'm sorry . . ." he told her.

She almost smiled. "No." She pressed a piece of paper with an address on it. "If you do find him."

"I can't," he told her, aware that his voice broke like a child's.

But she had turned and was walking away from him.

The boy with the glass eye never made it onto his examining table. Javier kept the piece of paper, folded neatly, in his wallet. Sometimes he would take it out and examine the spidery writing, the foreign address.

There were nights when the boy made it into his dreams, however, showing up unexpectedly on an examining table in Argentina or Rwanda. He would open the intact glass eye, like that of a Cyclops whose body had already disintegrated.

And he would tell the boy, in some surprise, "Your mother has been looking for you."

In the dream he would reach unsteadily into his wallet for the slip of paper, but it would be gone. He would empty the wallet onto a flat surface, shaking out credit cards and loose change, a dozen scraps of paper that he kept in the pockets of his billfold, pieces covered with names and addresses, but hers would not be among them.

"You look different," Alba told him upon his return.

And he had shrugged, reaching for her. "I'm tired."

"No, it's more than that," she insisted, but he had rested his fingers gently on her lips.

He gave her the cassette, together with the earrings. Sometimes they lay awake listening to the Ladino songs—love songs and lullabies, songs of parting. On nights when the sounds of Buenos Aires crept through the open windows, they provided accompaniment to the songs. The music inhabited the phantom space overhead.

We Will Sleep in One Nest*

OF ALL THE OBJECTS that we left behind, it is the paintings I miss most. Their oily smell finds me when I close my eyes and my fingers glide through the air as if sliding over their rough surfaces. I am strangely blinded upon opening my eyes—the white wall glares at me and I blink past its furious paleness.

When we were evacuated from Sarajevo, we were each allowed one bag to take on the bus. I watched my wife, Ruth, run around our house. First she filled a bag with photographs: yellowed shots of our wedding day in 1952, the children when they

*"*En un nido durmiremos . . .*" from "Una Noche al Lunar," a Ladino song from Sarajevo.

were small, grandchildren, graduations, birthdays. I was on the couch filling my pipe.

"Mordo"—her face was pale—"they won't all fit."

I rose and patted her arm. I hefted the bag in my hand. "This is no good," I told her. "We can't eat paper, and what if we have to run?"

I spied a photograph of myself on the top, a sharp nose pointing out beneath curly hair. "This is a horrible one of me, anyway." I smiled. "They'd never let me out of Sarajevo. They'd say, women and children, yes. Hedgehogs, no."

Ordinarily she would have laughed, but today my slight attempt at humor went unappreciated. Her face crumpled into tears and she sank into one of the chairs. "Our books, Mordo. What's going to happen to the books?"

My wife was a professor at Sarajevo University. I took her face in my hands, spectacles perched between us on the tip of her nose. Scraps of paper on which she had transcribed passages from favorite books lay scattered over every surface of furniture in our home like stray leaves. I was struck by how ill-equipped we were for the grimness of war.

I left her to sort underwear and sweaters, heels of bread and tins of food, and went up to the attic where I had my atelier. I sat on my stool and lit a cigarette, perhaps for the last time. Gauloises, they were from a carton my son had bought on the black market from a UN soldier.

"French?" I had asked him.

"The cigarettes or the soldier?"

I hazarded a guess. "Both?"

"Both," he confirmed.

"Ah well, let it never be said that we didn't do our part for the French economy," I told him glumly.

The cigarettes were strong even for my seasoned lungs, and as I lit one I looked through the burning smoke at the easel in front of me and at the half-finished portrait of my granddaughter.

I had stopped my "serious" painting, as my wife put it, some time ago. Gone were the abstracts, the bold departures into unknown territory. I had grown tired of experimentation in my old age, and drew instead things that pleased me. Faces I remembered from dreams. My wife's hip the morning after our first night together.

I had amused myself with drawing characters from the stories my granddaughter insisted upon hearing before sleep. Their wings and fantastic colors had kept me occupied for many weeks when I decided to paint her portrait.

I began drawing preliminary sketches of her during the final months of 1991. She had strained in her mother's lap as we tried to bribe her to stay still with sweets. She quieted only when she fell asleep, head tucked under her mother's chin, and we sat in the studio in silence, afraid of waking her. The sole noise was the grating of my charcoal against white paper and the occasional creak from my chair. Then the war started, and work on the portrait stopped. My granddaughter was half finished——a study in arrested development.

My daughter had comforted me. "Don't worry, Dad. She's growing so fast anyway. It's hard to keep up with her." It was true, every day her face had different lines and angles, her coloring changed just as my children's had.

Still, the half-finished painting bothered me. Her rosy face, where I had started to paint, was startling against the white and penciled lines of her undefined body. It was almost impossible to see the colorless landscape of her mother, the sketched lines were so faint.

I looked around the atelier. The afternoon light was fading fast and would soon cast deep shadows across the dusty corners where canvases leaned against the wall. We had long ago removed the lightbulb and used it elsewhere in the house for those times when we had electricity. I could take a candle up to the studio, but what was the use?

I got up and started to shuffle canvases.

Hana, my first wife, had been from an old, affluent Ladino family in Sarajevo. Her father had commissioned me, then a student at the Academy, to paint her portrait under the watchful eye of her grandmother. The old woman was not the chaperone I would have chosen. She had the unfortunate habit of falling asleep, leaving us free to whisper back and forth, stopping in mid-sentence when the old woman stirred. I worked at a leisurely pace, drawing and erasing and drawing again.

"But it's fine!" her mother would remark about my progress, bewildered.

"No!" I would tell her in an agitated tone, playing the artist. I ripped up preliminary sketches five times, insisting, "No, it must be perfect. Perfection requires time," and would turn to see Hana with a hand over her mouth, hiding a smile.

But I was looking for a different portrait now. That first portrait of Hana had turned to ash fifty years ago, as our parents had. As had Hana and our only child, a daughter.

I finally found what I was looking for behind more recent efforts, and slid it out carefully. Time had not dulled the rich blackness of her hair, or the arching brows, and I sat looking at her smile. As in my granddaughter's portrait, her face had been one of the only painted sections, where I had started to add color over the penciled lines of the drawing underneath. I had always been stubborn, starting my paintings from the point at which convention and Academy teachers dictated I should not. Previously the background had hung grayly behind her, as if she were seated among clouds. In my worst moments, they were wisps of smoke.

But when I returned from the camp in 1945 and liberated the painting from my old professor's office, where I had left it for safekeeping, I carried it home to a space graced neither by wife nor by child. One night, when I had drunk the silence back with a bottle of *rakija*, I drew my chair up to the painting and started to paint a crude fire in the lower-right-hand corner of the canvas. Its tongues licked furiously and perversely at Hana's bare arms. The baby's face had been almost obliterated by the orange and red paint, and I sat there crying, looking at my burning wife and child.

The next morning I had risen painfully, rubbing my head. The picture sickened me. It was the only likeness I had of them. All the photographs were missing, and I imagined them flying through the city like confetti, stomped into the snow by the indifferent feet of pedestrians. I had ruined that picture of them, of our domestic peace. I had dragged them squarely into the arena of war.

I attempted other pictures of them. I closed my eyes and beheld them like a candle whose flame I was coaxing to life. Opening my eyes extinguished it every time. I tried everything: sketching with my eyes closed, only to find some woman who bore no resemblance to my Hana. I got drunk, drawing the bitter dark into my belly, and painted for hours. On those nights, I went to bed happy, sure that I had gotten her this time, certain that her features were imprinted in my heart as if etched there by steel chisels. And each time, morning brought the taste of bile, the dismay of gazing on a face that, while pretty enough, was not my wife's. *Where are you?* I would ask the canvas, as if the real Hana would rise to the surface like a swimmer. I asked the air, which was empty and strange. I stopped trying to paint her, because my efforts drove her ever further away.

The next morning I rose hours before Ruth and watched her sleep for a moment before slipping out of the room and back to the attic. When we decided to marry, I drew a line on the pavement with a white stone and took her hand, saying, "This, Ruth, is where the future starts." We jumped over the line, her hand in mine. But it was not a sealed border, and Hana was always there. Still, I do not think that Ruth ever blamed me for it.

My granddaughter's portrait was still on the easel and I set about completing it, quickly and sloppily. When I had finished, I sat back and looked. The colors were dismally wrong and the body out of proportion. It was worse than my earliest juvenile efforts, but I was satisfied. I cleaned the brushes, and soaked them in turpentine as if I believed I would really return.

I rubbed my hands with a turpentine-soaked cloth, the familiar heavy smell rising to my nostrils and coating my hand like a comforting, albeit caustic, grease.

When I left, I looked back, my foot on the top step. Her face was like a tiny winter sun that did not burn, but warmed my back as I departed.

Later, when we were already living by the sea in our Makarska hotel as refugees, a friend's son sent back word from Sarajevo that a shell had crashed through the roof of our house and the whole place had burned to a black skeleton.

"The turpentine," I told my wife sadly. "The turpentine and the oils would have made all the paintings go up quickly."

"Maybe something survived," she said, trying to comfort me. "Canvas and scraps of paper here and there."

"No, no." I smiled. "It will all be gone now."

Our daughter went to Israel with her family, our unmarried son to America. They are both trying to persuade us to come and live with them, but we are too tired. The prospect of new places and new languages makes us nervous. Besides, we are like homing pigeons; we always return sooner or later, in one form or another.

A few months ago, an American art historian came to visit me. A former student of mine, now an assistant lecturer at a small American university, had referred him to me.

The man came asking questions about the Sarajevo Haggadah. They wanted to make a television documentary about it and were trying to track it down. Might I know where it was?

I was somewhat amused. I was a Jew from Sarajevo and an artist, but not necessarily an expert in these matters. "No, I don't know where it is," I told him. "But I've been told that it's quite safe."

"But the bombing and the rockets. It could go up in flames." He was perturbed, and I looked at him steadily.

"What do you suggest?" I asked him. "A convoy? A rescue operation?"

He looked at me blankly, not sure if I was making fun of him, and we spoke of other things for a while.

But since then I have been thinking about the Haggadah. And about my paintings. Perhaps there is some corner of the city where they are miraculously preserved. It is true, I have been told the Haggadah is safe.

My daughter holds my granddaughter up to the phone when they call from Israel. I think that she is beginning to forget us. She has most certainly forgotten her city.

"*Nono,*" she says shrilly, "Mama won't give me chocolate . . ." I begin to laugh.

". . . and I must go to bed early. Too early. Tell her not to make me."

"I made her go to bed early when she was your age," I tell her seriously. "It is an injustice we all commit against our young."

But the child has already returned the receiver to her mother's hand and I can hear her shrieking in the background, running through the apartment, overturning furniture and laughing.

"You wouldn't recognize her, Dad," my daughter tells me, and I am stabbed by something, by some shard of a dusty January day in a landscape I have not seen for some time. We say goodbye and silence closes over the miles of telephone wire between us.

My first daughter had turned one the day I started the sketches. Hana placed her on her knee as if the baby were riding a pony and bounced her. The child grabbed Hana's hair to steady herself and we laughed at her fiercely clenched fists.

Hana gently unclenched the baby's hands and kissed both palms. The baby laughed and laughed. Her laughing washed over my face as if I were underwater, sending ripples and waves which rocked the surface. Her laughter climbed in through my ears and lowered itself into my limbs. So that I could hear her laughing, even as the red fires covered her.

Where None
Is the Number

THEY CALLED HIM BOSTON. It was not the nom de guerre he would have chosen for himself. It passed from man to man, the faintest exhalation of breath and the hissing *s* spreading horizontally like wind, and he grinned that such a name might be his only legacy in this place. The city of his birth did not even begin to explain him, though eventually he came to appreciate the irony.

He had seen it used in a cable once, the one word identifiable in a morass of language he only marginally understood. A strange feeling had started at the base of his spine when he saw the blunt block lettering. BOSTON. The name was an anchor, something familiar in alien surroundings, but it had grown steadily less recognizable. Soon it did not so much suit him as it chafed him, and he accepted this as his first lesson of war. It came to him one night in his grandfather's voice as he nosed around the edges of sleep. *Long-held truths are the first to go.*

He could imagine the cable they would send to his mother in America if he died. *Vaš sin Boston je mrtav.* She wouldn't know what to make of that message, and would file it absentmindedly with her shopping receipts and pay stubs, wondering all the while when her son would be returning home.

They had suggested he not carry identification on the front line. At first he had liked the anonymity; in his fatigues and with his mouth shut, he had the same skin as all the other men. Only his shock of red hair differentiated him, as it did everywhere. But a few days on the line had remedied even this, fading the color to an indistinct reddish brown.

After a few weeks of seeing men killed, however, when it was not always possible to reach the bodies and they had to be left behind, the implications of anonymity sank in. He could picture her seated in the red linoleum kitchen, unchanged since his childhood, waiting.

He made his commanding officer memorize his name. *Antonio Murphy.* It was a ridiculous name, he was forced to admit. He could not help but smile each time it was called out with others: *Marković, Matić, Murphy, Novosel.* The Irish-Portuguese mix was the same name printed on the ID card he stubbornly began to carry. But like Boston, it seemed less familiar with each passing day. He pulled the ID out when he was alone. The plastic rectangle covering it became so scratched and clouded that the red-haired man in the photograph appeared to be backing away from a window.

At first they did not trust him. There was a shortage of weapons, and he was not immediately given a gun. Even when a sad assortment was delivered to the unit, they were distributed to others first. In those early evenings as they cleaned their arms, he brought out a knife and whetstone. He was not sure the blade would do him any good—it seemed small defense from machine guns and falling shells—but the action of sharpening it soothed him. *Preparation, Readiness, Discipline.* The old man had told him on more than one occasion that these were the marks of a good soldier.

He kept the knife honed to a razor sharpness, so that it scored the inside of its leather sheath, its metal tip coming to rest against the metal guard. He was struck by its reflective surface each time he removed it. His reverie and the subsequent scraping sound of stone on metal initially brought the measured glances of other men.

"Cool cat, eh, Boston?" Someone asked him the second night, coming over and extending a hand. The man explained that he had returned because of the war. He spoke a strange, accented Australian vernacular that made the American smile. "My name is Miki."

Later, when he was issued a decrepit rifle, he kept the knife in his boot. A gun could become jammed or misfire, but the knife's properties were fixed. It was a family heirloom of sorts. His grandfather had carried it in the Second World War, and his father in Vietnam. He showed Miki where their initials were carved into the hilt.

Like his fellow combatants, he took advantage of the weeks they rotated off the line to write to his family. "Dear Granddad and Mom," he began each letter home. "Have you been lighting candles for me at St. Catherine's?"

At first his mother had believed he was hiking through Europe, philosophical if unusual therapy after breaking up with his girlfriend. Few people from their working-class neighborhood went to Europe, much less hiked across it, but she took it in stride. Her boy had always been different.

He had quit his job, readied supplies, and bought a one-way airline ticket to London. His mother had driven him to the airport, her sad Portuguese eyes tearing on the way. "She was never for you," she told him, finally, standing awkwardly outside the terminal. "That girl was like cheap fabric."

His mother had worked in a garment factory in her youth and had an uncanny knack for thinking in terms of that industry. He had grinned and kissed her cheek, slinging his bag over one shoulder. He never bothered to explain that the breakup had been his decision, that he was tired of his girlfriend's chatter and that he had grown even more tired of his life. He was almost thirty and had never been challenged. He knew that each man had a quest in front of him, but he decided there was no use in waiting for one to present itself.

Granddad had been somewhat savvier. The son of an Irish fisherman, he had sharp black eyes that missed nothing. On Sundays when Antonio went over to his mother's house, he would sit watching television with his grandfather after dinner. Soccer or football some days, but increasingly toward the end it had been news. There were stories of a buildup to war. Republics he knew little enough about were declaring independence from a country he could only barely locate on a map.

"Look at that!" His grandfather would point at tanks moving on the screen. When the sieges of cities in eastern Croatia began a few weeks later, his grandfather beat his cane on the parquet floor. "If I were a younger man . . ." he muttered to himself.

His grandfather had theories of a greater Catholic brother-hood. Sure, these people had been Commies for years, he explained to his grandson, but underneath it all they were still children of Rome. Antonio had not stepped into a church for years and had few opinions on the subject, but something about the footage made him sit up and take notice.

His mother had been summoned from the kitchen by the tapping cane, and stood behind her father-in-law's chair, drying her hands on her apron. "Poor people," she said to no one in particular. "Poor, poor people."

Antonio had followed the beginning of the siege almost obsessively, sifting his way through conflicting news reports. Two weeks later, when he announced over Sunday dinner that he had left his job and was going to take a trip, his mother chewed thoughtfully, then declared it a good way to get his mind off things. His grandfather had said nothing, but his eyes seemed to leave singe marks on Antonio's face. He reddened and looked away. After dinner, his grandfather pulled from under his bed the shoe box which contained the handful of his son's possessions, sent back from Vietnam in plastic, and removed the knife.

He arrived before the fall of Vukovar, although he was not sent there. Instead, he was kept in Zagreb for several weeks. They did not know what to do with him, and suggested he return home. A harried-looking colonel who had owned a dry cleaning business in Chicago barked in his face, "What the hell we gonna do with you?"

"Send me to fight."

The colonel eyed him sternly. "You think this is some kind of game? You wanna commit suicide?"

Antonio shook his head.

The man thought a moment before asking his next question. "You a crazy?"

He had almost laughed. No, he said, he was no crazy.

"Why you come, then? Your people aren't even from here."

Antonio's shoulders twitched.

"Your shrug not going to mean much out there. That's not going to save you." The colonel looked at the cross around his neck and pointed to it. "That's not going to save you, either. Believe me. I seen a lot of those lately, but they just get buried, too."

They stared at each other across the desk.

"Fine," the older man said, slamming one of his desk drawers.

And so they gave him a uniform, and he joined a unit in Slavonia where men regarded him with perplexed eyes, patted his back, and called him Boston.

Early in his life, Antonio discovered that everything he touched seemed to turn out wrong.

As a teenager, he and his friends started breaking into abandoned houses, storage units, and cars. He never stole anything, just looked through the merchandise, sat on people's sofas, or drove the cars around for a while. He became adept at picking locks and his friends dared him to ever riskier ventures. He was caught only once, while hot-wiring a ten-year-old Ford. One moment he was aware of his friends egging him on, the next of their rapid retreat. In the rearview mirror, he saw the black-and-white pull up. By the time they turned on their flashing lights he had decided to sit still. He spent several hours in a holding cell at the police station, answering questions in monosyllables.

"You don't care much, do you?" one of the policemen asked him, putting down his pencil. "What the hell is wrong with you, kid?"

Not even the sight of his mother's tearstained face had been enough to bring him out of his trance, and he sat silently as she expounded his virtues: ". . . never been in trouble before . . . a good boy, just confused." And their predicament: "His father died. It's just me and his granddad raising him . . ."

His grandfather was so upset that he slapped Antonio and had some kind of fit afterward. The old man shook all over, dropped into a chair, and his eyes rolled back into his head. When he regained consciousness, he found his grandson pulling on his arms and weeping.

They sat for some moments, white-lipped and staring at one another. Then his granddad rose shakily and showed him the shoe box under the bed, the treasure trove of his only son. "Your father," he told Antonio, "was a hero. That places a certain responsibility on your shoulders."

And he removed the letters, folded into squares, from the bottom of the box and handed them to his grandson. Antonio retired to his room with them, not emerging until he had read them all. They formed a record from basic training to a week before his death. "Dear Dad," they began, in a script he had never seen, but which was achingly familiar. "Have you been lighting candles for me at St. Catherine's?"

———————

Miki was shot in the thigh and sent off the line to recuperate. A few days later, shrapnel hit Antonio in the back, and he was also sent off the line. In the seconds after it happened, he thought that his back was on fire and rolled from side to side in the grass trying to extinguish it.

"You okay!" they shouted at him. "Boston, you okay!"

Initially he thought they were asking him, and he stared at the circle of faces around him dumbly, then realized they were telling him.

He was bored in the hospital and wrote a long letter to his mother. She had already discovered his subterfuge weeks before. He had even called her once from a post office when they were off the line.

"I don't understand. You grew up in Somerville, for Christ's sake," she had told him the first time, crying. "You sound like somebody else," she said accusingly. "I want my son back, damn it. I lost your father. Isn't that enough?"

He heard her take a shuddering breath and he stiffened in the post office cabin, brushing the wooden sides with his fingertips. He was learning just enough Croatian to make out that Inga loved Tomislav, and that Zdenka was a whore.

He heard his mother hand the phone to his grandfather. "You there, boy?" the old man asked him, his voice tight.

"I'm here, Granddad." But his voice sounded remote now. The sealed wooden booth vibrated, making the skin on his arms crawl, and he broke the connection before hearing what the old man had to say.

When he called them a second time, from the hospital, his

grandfather told him to come home. "Enough now, boy. You proved yourself. Time to come home, don't you think?"

He wondered idly if this was true, but then changed the subject.

"There are other letters, you know," his mother told him when she came to the phone. "From your father. Letters I never showed you or your granddad, letters he sent to me. He wouldn't like what you're doing, not one bit."

But her words were only glancing blows.

He returned to his ward and spent a long time staring at a blank piece of paper before beginning to write to his mother. *There comes a time each man must make sense of the reason he exists*, he wrote to her. He remembered a Dylan song she used to sing him when he was little, and hummed a few bars under his breath. *Where have you been, my blue-eyed son?* He thought of it as a hippie song, and he could imagine his mother dressed in Indian print dresses, pregnant and waiting for his father to return.

He paraphrased the song: *I'm going out before it starts raining again.* The words looked ridiculously random on the page, and he wasn't at all sure she would understand the reference. He added, *I'm sorry.*

When he recovered, they sent him to the front behind Zadar, where life consisted of war, blinding white stone, and rare glimpses of the sea. When he was off the front line he did what other men in the unit did: played cards, drank, slept. He even had a girlfriend, a tall black-haired girl named Iva. He called her Evie, which made her laugh. She gave him a white crystal rosary which he wore around his neck.

His unit began to think that he was lucky, though others grumbled that he was merely reckless. After his first injury, he seemed untouchable. He could stand upright behind their positions and not get shot, but a moment later, if someone else ventured a look, a bullet would find its mark.

"I don't understand it," Miki would say in amazement, looking at his friend's flaming hair. He had returned after Boston, and the two had become inseparable. "With your head, it should be like a flare."

And Boston would shrug. "Luck of the Portuguese-Irish, I guess."

He began volunteering for things to test this newfound power. He discovered, to his surprise, that he could run through a hail of bullets and not one would touch him. He could drive a car down a mined road and suffer nothing worse than a flat tire.

"Aren't you ever afraid, Boston?" Miki asked him. "Don't you ever want to go home and start a life?"

Antonio did not respond. How to explain that his life had started here? That Boston had ceased to exist as a physical place altogether. That he was strangely at peace in chaos. It was the hum of the everyday that frightened him now.

Miki was silent for a moment before answering his own question. "I want to go back to my father's town and help him run his farm. I want to find a girl and screw a lot—"

And Antonio had shushed him. His friend's words pierced him, and he wondered for a moment if he was jealous. The future was no more. Or, more accurately, he was no more in it. He could no longer bear to think of his mother, of the house where he had grown up, of what he would do afterward. Afterward opened its

mouth like a whale, and he could see nothing but its black and in-
finite belly.

The future was forbidden, he told Miki tersely, if either expected to make it out alive.

Two days later Miki was shot through the head by a sniper. Boston
turned and screamed in the direction of the shot. "Shoot me!" he
yelled at the unseen gunman. "Shoot me, too!" He rose to his feet
and jumped around, waving his hands, as other men yelled at him
to get down.

His CO's voice was louder than the rest. He threatened to
shoot Antonio himself if he did not get behind a barrier.

Boston threw his friend over his shoulder and went uselessly
in search of a medic. He could feel the blood dripping onto his
Achilles tendon. It made a rhythm that echoed in his head for days.

He stopped writing home and stopped telephoning. Other friends
came and went. They were both more and less than brothers to
him. And with each day it seemed that he closed in on some
greater truth, that he could almost taste it like a mint between his
teeth.

His luck held, but after Miki died, he realized that there was a
strange mirror play at work: no bullet touched him, but death and
destruction seemed to doggedly pursue him.

Evie was not immune. On the night he hurried to the bus stop
which was their rendezvous to tell her that he was a curse and he
could no longer see her, a driver lost contol of his car and plowed
into the bench where she sat. Cresting a hill, Boston saw it unfold
in front of him. He shouted and for a moment it seemed that Evie

raised her head and smiled before she was enveloped by the car moving fast upon her in a shudder of breaking glass and bending metal.

He sat with members of her family in their cold refugee quarters at the Hotel Kolovare in Zadar after the funeral. Her mother wept while she made coffee on an electric hot plate. When she handed it to him, it tasted like salt, and he drank it in one swig.

Did her daughter suffer?

He knew enough Croatian to understand the question. *No*, he managed to convey, *Evie didn't even see anything coming.* Through the window he saw a bird wheeling over the sea dive suddenly like a dart to pluck some dark and wriggling thing from the gray water.

He began spending most of his time alone. At night he would not sleep in a foxhole or a barracks with other men, and no one objected.

At some point he made the decision to move on to Bosnia. His luck had come to infuriate him. It made him miserable, kept him alive, but would not allow him companionship of any kind. If there was one place to test your luck, he thought, it was in Bosnia, where life was reputed to be dirt-cheap. Initial fighting between the Serbs and other Bosnians had degenerated still further, and now chaos reigned. Croatians and Moslems, former allies, were fighting each other.

His CO had tried to explain to him who was to blame for this factionalism. "Bosnia, she has always been a problem. Herzegovina, too. But we have to fight for our brothers. You understand? It comes down to that."

But he had not understood. How could the enemy suddenly change faces? How could allies, even uneasy ones, turn on one another?

"It is not so clear-cut," the older man had told him patiently. "It is not so clean."

He had remained obstinately silent.

"Take Vukovar, for example."

There was grumbling among the fighters. *Vukovar was sold,* they claimed. *Vukovar was ceded by the authorities in distant Zagreb in a cynical trade that sacrified one city for another.* He did not believe it.

"You're naïve," Miki had told him affectionately before his death. "You want to believe that people are good."

He made his way to Mostar, this time as a civilian, where the Neretva River split the population between the Croatian west and Moslem east. He visited Stari Most, the bridge and architectural marvel which spanned the Neretva River. He never made it onto the bridge but viewed it from beneath at night, from the vantage point of the right bank. By moonlight he carved his own initials into the knife's hilt and dropped it into the river. Five days later the bridge was blown up, all that perfectly hewn stone crashing into the water like lead.

The Croatian side was responsible and a stiff figure on television called the bridge a strategic target. For days he woke to the sound of its falling pieces.

The woman he was paying by the day for a drafty room removed every image of the bridge from her home. Ink drawings and painted ceramic plates had graced each wall.

He found an English-speaking priest who agreed to hear his confession.

"Why?" Antonio asked near tears, the wooden kneeler biting into his legs. "Why has everything turned out this way?"

He could see the man go tense through the grille of the confessional, and explained about Miki and Evie. He told the priest about his grandfather and the box at home. There was the faint sound of a distant explosion outside.

"What do you think has guided you here?" the priest asked finally.

Antonio shook his head. "To confession?" He could see the priest lean forward.

"To the war. Why is it that you have come?"

Antonio considered for a moment. *Religion*, he wanted to say. Or, *a desire to do good*. He tested the word *boredom* on his tongue but did not like its sound, nor that of *a family tradition*.

Nothing seemed worth saying and he sat uncomfortably as the priest prescribed his penance, a handful of prayers Antonio had long ago forgotten and had no interest in reciting.

It seemed to him when he left the church that his father's ghost walked out in front of him. Antonio let it go, ashamed.

He decided, then, to leave. He made his way back to Zagreb, where the colonel watched him strangely and returned the passport in his safekeeping. He placed it together with the ID card, so scratched and beaten that the photograph seemed to depict nothing in particular and the name was barely legible.

He bought a plane ticket from Munich, not trusting his luck to hitchhike back to England. He could imagine the mayhem of pileups and tunnel explosions he would trail like a bloody wake behind him.

He was on edge during the flight, expecting the plane to crash, leaving him the sole survivor bobbing in gray and unforgiving waves. But the plane did not encounter so much as a patch of turbulence.

Upon arrival at Logan Airport, the passport official glanced at him coolly. He no longer resembled his passport photo. "What were you doing abroad?" he asked.

"Hiking," he told the man. "Backpacking."

"For two years?"

He looked at the man in some surprise.

"Anything to declare?" they asked him in the customs line.

"Nothing." He had just a duffel bag, and they glanced at it cursorily before waving him through.

Outside, he went to a pay phone and called his mother collect. Car horns blared behind him, and the smell of exhaust was dizzying. Her voice was ethereal to him, and when he replaced the receiver he spent long moments examining his battered hand, willing it to unclench from the scratched black plastic. She was there in record time, one side of her head done up in curlers. She jumped out of the car, leaving the engine running. When she caught sight of him, she burst into tears, leaning her forehead on the top of the car. Arriving passengers were beginning to stare, and a policeman was moving purposefully toward them.

He steered his mother to the passenger side of the car and tossed his duffel in the back. He threw the car into gear and drove in the direction of home.

His grandfather was dead, she told him in half sentences through tears. "So worried . . . I never forgave him. Never forgave himself!"

For days afterward he waited for lightning to strike their house or for the furnace to explode. Each time his mother went out to do shopping, he expected that she would not come back, but each time she returned. After a month, he sighed in relief, believing the spell broken.

He went to visit his grandfather's grave, burying Evie's rosary beside it.

His mother had not lied. She did indeed have her own set of letters from his father, and they revealed a different man from the one in his granddad's shoe box. Each brave letter had its meeker twin, and he matched them side by side.

Forgive me, sweet girl, for putting this all on you . . . can only think of you, but mustn't. It's the only way through . . . Nothing is worth anything . . . I came with the belief in the value of things . . .

And then, the last one, dated a few days before his death. *I believe that I will never die.*

And Boston sat shivering at the kitchen table, the letters strewn on the red linoleum surface in front of him, wondering if he was there at all. Wondering if, in some alternate universe, he was not leading a life in which his father had died of old age and in which he himself was something altogether different.

Or maybe they were all dead, it occurred to him as he began scooping up the letters. His hands were gray, and he made a pile of the paper squares, retying the frayed ribbon around the bunch. There was comfort in that.

Swimming Out

MY BROTHER, Željko, died by the sea.

A man from his unit described it to us two weeks ago: *We were on a peak behind Dubrovnik. It was freezing, wind screaming through the rocks like some crazy woman. We were hunkered down and playing cards. When the shelling began I dove right and Željko dove left—*

He died five years ago but we had never heard the details. I came home to do so, catching an overnight bus from Zagreb. I was trying to look serene while listening to the man, but something caught my attention. There was a school picture of my brother on the credenza behind our visitor, and my eyes met my brother's in the instant I learned how he had died.

Željko grinned from photographs in every room of our childhood home. Months ago I found a box of milk teeth in my
mother's bedside table. They were Željko's and mine, tiny, white,
and indistinguishable. When the box was shaken, they made a
sound like a rattle filled with beads.

He died in full view of the sea, the man from his unit added after
an uncomfortable silence, a tremor climbing into his voice as wind
into water. The knowledge entered me like a burrowing animal
and has been carving a tunnel from one limb to another, crossing
and recrossing, ever since.

A cup of coffee grew cold on his knee, his legs jutting awkwardly from his seated position on my parents' couch, as he tried
unsuccessfully to meet our eyes. There was no recrimination from
my parents, whose only son was decomposing in the village cemetery while this man sat intact in their home. I did not start wailing,
pounding his chest with my clenched fists. I gave him no opportunity to take them gently in his hands and comfort me. In truth, I
think that he was somewhat disappointed by this.

Željko talked about you so much I feel I know you, Maja, he said as
I walked him out to his car. While I absentmindedly watched it recede down the road, I remembered something my mother had
told me after I questioned her about the milk teeth. *When Željko
was born, the first thing I did was trace the lines on his fingers and toes.*

Indoors, I helped mechanically clear the table, whisking away
all traces of our visitor. But one notion consumed me: the sea, the
same sea in which we played as children, had betrayed us.

Željko's friend gave me the idea of a pilgrimage, and for the past
two weeks nothing else has interested me. This morning I called

the office were I work, pretending to be sick. "A bug," I told the receptionist.

She clucked her tongue sympathetically. "You poor dear," she told me.

I have not explained the trip to my parents or to the aunt with whom I live in Zagreb. I spoke only vaguely of needing some time alone, away from the city. I have little idea what I will do once I reach Dubrovnik, or what I expect to find there.

When I arrive at the bus station, I could swear that there is a flicker of recognition on the ticket seller's face as she shoves my change into the tray between us, but then she looks over my shoulder and calls, "Next!"

And as I board the bus, I pretend I am visiting a new lover. He would be a likable man but someone I do not love. There have been plenty of those in recent months, as the blue shadows beneath my eyes attest. I know that mine is a life lived out of balance, but for the sake of my mission I forgive myself for past indiscretions, for reproaching every whole young man. I see them hurrying to work in the mornings, looking smart in suits their mothers and wives have pressed for them. They fill Zagreb's cafés and wink at me conspiratorially, offering to buy me drinks. And I hate them all, because Željko should be among them.

I powder the shadows of my face with the compact from my purse and sigh inwardly, aware of the distance speeding beneath us.

When I lean my face against the window, Zagreb's southern neighborhoods unwind beneath my cheek. The National Library rises before me, a large glass-and-chrome cube in a field of low-flung buildings. Its opening had been anxiously anticipated several years before. Newspapers cited the powerful lines of its architecture as proof of the nation's modernity. *War cannot stop progress,* the building proclaimed to an ambivalent sky.

The library had been moved from a smaller, older structure in the center of town across from the Botanical Gardens. I remember trips to the city as a child when Željko and I sat quietly in the reading room, swinging our legs and looking at the stained-glass window in the ceiling while our father pored over a collection of musty-smelling books.

I prefer the imperfection of the buildings across the street from the new library, rickety paint-peeled structures with tiny windows, tilting against one another like drunken men staggering home. Instead of the cold edges of a modern building, there is the occasional brown and twisting vine, the sheets that hang on lines, worn so thin in places that they appear as flimsy and damp as breath.

An artificial breeze blows from tiny overhead nozzles. I raise a hand to test the coolness with my fingers and adjust the nozzle so that it points away from me. Summer is slowly being dislodged by encroaching fall.

I know that I am fickle. In a few months I will long for the heat, summoning its memory and subtracting its discomfort. The smell of sun on the city's metal and cinder blocks will be sweeter, to say nothing of the sun on pine.

I have not answered the phone since returning to the city. I had been convinced for so long that when carving a hole in the body, you must pack it with something to stop the flow of blood. But since Željko's friend came to my parents' house, I have let it bleed in waves.

My aunt has been taking messages which she delivers with a

worried face. "No," I hear her tell first one, then another, "Maja's not here."

When the bus turns onto the southern highway to the sea I am almost asleep. My hands rest lightly in my lap, palms upward, a patina of dust giving them the appearance of clay. The mountains are the last obstruction to the coast, and by the time we reach them I dream of walking beneath the sea.

My brother is gone. I am here, for now, hanging by a thread.

When Željko was alive, he was fiercely protective of me. In his absence I find myself making unwise decisions.

My modus operandi does not vary. The first time I meet them, I ask if they follow politics.

They usually make a face. "Boring" is their stock reply.

And in a way, I am relieved.

"Where were you during the war?" I will prod.

Some have the grace to redden.

The last one, a businessman, confessed, "My parents helped send me away. I was in Italy the entire time."

And although they frequently discover my circumstances, they never broach the subject of the brother whom they will never meet.

As an act of revenge, I forget their names quickly.

I display no surfeit of emotion with men now. I marvel at myself, at how bland my face can become when we drive through the center of town in their luxury sedans. I would nod on cue when the businessman told me about his day, about how business was going and about the girls who worked behind the counter in his stores. He confided which were the best saleswomen and which he would have to fire. He brought me French perfumes and scented creams which I rubbed obligingly into my neck and hands.

But it has been a few weeks now since I returned his phone calls. At first he had been persistent. I would hear his angry voice through the receiver as my aunt spoke to him. And then the calls tapered off, like the others.

"Maja!" my aunt told me fiercely. "This is a city where people talk." She wanted to say, *I know it's not easy on you with your brother dead, but first that crazy Luka and now this litany of men!*

When I awake, an old woman is sitting in the seat beside me, eating a mealy pear with a paring knife. I shake my head when I am offered a piece and the woman shrugs.

"Are you going on vacation?" she asks, taking the slice of pear between her own yellowed teeth.

I straighten self-consciously. "I'm going to visit a friend."

The woman nods. "You won't be needing a room, then," she says matter-of-factly. The black eyes that meet mine are calculating. "I rent rooms on the sea. Very cheap."

"No." I shake my head, and look out the window.

After a moment, the old woman nudges my arm. "Is it a woman that you're going to see, or a man?"

Ghosts, I want to tell her, but instead I respond with an unfriendly stare. I allow my face to fall into expressionless lines, eyes like two opaque pebbles. I have been practicing this art for months.

"It's just that I have a special rate for two people. Very romantic and lots of privacy."

I ignore her and she shrugs a second time, busying herself with the plastic bag at her feet. She pulls out a gossip magazine I recognize as one my aunt reads. I remember that the final page is an advice column for women whose husbands ignore them, beat them, or will not leave them alone in bed. There is a photograph of the woman who answers their letters, oval eyeglasses and a frozen smile above her column to reassure her unsettled flock.

The bus shivers underneath me as I read over the woman's shoulder. *Without love, every woman is adrift.*

I wonder what the magazine columnist would have advised regarding Luka.

In his late thirties, he was older than I by more than ten years. He was also from the country, although years of residence in the city had made his accent less clipped than mine. In his better moments he would rest his head upon my stomach, close his eyes, and tell me that I sounded like home.

The independent newspaper where he worked gave his byline from the capital, although he filed his articles from various locations. During the war he had reported from the trenches, first from Croatia and then from the densely wooded hills of Bosnia. He would return to Zagreb for scant hours of sleep, shedding his Kevlar and muddy boots.

I had not known him then and was therefore unable to assess how the war had changed him.

"Better that you didn't," he had told me once, magnanimously. "You romanticize everything and are usually disappointed."

His temper was legendary, and he had nearly been fired several times because of it.

"Our best correspondent, but a mouth like a machine gun," his editor told me at a dinner, and then, after a pause, "But who'd be normal after all of that?"

Luka grew particularly agitated when conversations touched on the war. He detested the official line, finding fault at every turn. When Bosnia came up, he would begin to rant. He had been ejected from several bars in town after drinking too much and getting into arguments. With growing frequency, he would appear in the middle of the night at my apartment wincing and holding a bloody Kleenex to his nose.

It was when he was drinking that his accent became more pronounced, despite the incoherencies he would mutter when I brought a blanket with which to cover him on the couch. Then, grabbing my arms, he would suddenly become lucid, telling me about the siege. About the cameraman in front of him.

"His name was Željko," he would tell me. "Like your brother."

"I know," I would respond tiredly. "You've told me."

"The sniper must have seen the camera. The bullet went through the camera before it went through his head." Sometimes he told me about the way the cameraman fell, so slowly that it happened as in a dream. Other times he would describe the color of his blood.

"Different," he would tell me, beginning to shiver. "It's somehow a different color when it comes from the head."

Sometimes he sent furniture flying, leaving me to sweep up splinters of wood and glass. The woman who lived next door would pound on the walls, shrieking and threatening to call the police.

My friends did not understand my patience. "It's just furniture now," one said, "but you haven't got an endless supply."

When he fell asleep, I would stay, watching him. My lover. My brother's posthumous biographer.

Before I left for the bus station this morning, my aunt puttered around the kitchen making grim predictions. She was unhappy about my trip to the sea. She felt sure that I was planning to meet someone. "One of *them*," she said disdainfully. Their cars with their engines that hum soundlessly leave her cold. She finds their displays of wealth undignified. "This one doesn't go to church," or, "That one's from the city, and God knows who his people are."

She does not know about my war of attrition, and so I merely smiled.

"Everything amuses you these days," my aunt snapped. "Everything is funny."

"No"—I looked into the bottom of my coffee cup—"nothing is funny these days." But the smile remained.

"How long will you be gone?" she asked finally, throwing a washcloth into the sink, where it wrapped around the faucet with a wet slapping sound. She sat down beside me, wiping the palms of her hands on the faded black dress.

"A few days," I told her.

She shook her head, tapping the tabletop with her palm. A few strands of steely hair stuck out at her temples like coiling wire, and I lifted a hand to tuck them beneath the kerchief covering her hair.

My brother and I had lived with her while we studied in the city. We shared a room, and I would cover for him when he came in late from drinking with his friends. Looking around the kitchen this morning, I remembered sitting there with him, making faces at each other behind our aunt's back. He would not have approved of my current situation, of my men or of the thread by which I hang. I wonder what he would have made of Luka.

My aunt was watching me closely. She had liked Luka for the most part. But the morning I appeared with my suitcases and a box of books, she had taken one look at my face and began to curse his entire lineage. *Don't worry, Maja,* she had told me, *you'll find someone better.*

I reminded her of that pronouncement this morning. "I can't spend my life in mourning," I said. My smile, eroding steadily, felt like something a taxidermist would have to shoot full of poisons to preserve.

"Fine." My aunt reached over mechanically to pour more coffee from the brass pot. But I could see that she was not concentrating because sludge from the bottom of the pot fell thickly into my cup. And I was not concentrating either, because when I lifted it to my lips I ended up with a mouthful of thick bitterness, the tiny splinters coating my tongue like sand.

It is to another picture of Luka that I have clung foolishly for months, clipped like a photograph and fading in my wallet.

The war was over. The third anniversary of my brother's death had come and gone, an event for which I had returned dutifully to my parents' home.

I had accompanied my mother to the cemetery, helping tidy the gravestone. While my mother rubbed the dark granite with a cloth, I arranged flowers in the urn by the stone which contained my brother's name. We lit the candles together.

On the last day of my visit, my mother blew her nose into a

handkerchief and we stood silently for several moments. "I predict good things for you this year, Maja," she told me.

And I leaned over to place a kiss on my mother's cheek, the stone hills rising behind us, blue and hard, a monument to a life given and confiscated. In the black-and-white landscape, they provided the only color in my days there.

Back in Zagreb, the grayness continued its steady contagion. Until one evening when I met friends at a noisy café in town. Men at the next table were arguing about the war.

"It *is* a fucking mess!" One voice rose above the others.

"Keep your voice down." His companion's tones were low and reasonable.

But the first man continued, "We fed them to bursting with patriotism . . . pipe dreams . . . carted them off because of ego. They died and others became rich . . . Don't give me the fucking success of our offensive when I remember the beginning." The voice became a shout and I turned to watch the man who was talking. Blue-black stubble covered his cheeks and he had an angular, wolflike face.

"Let's go, Maja." One of my friends was watching me anxiously, but I ignored her.

" . . . and it meant nothing."

With those words, anger drove through my rib cage like a stake. I rose to my feet and lurched over to the table. The man continued to talk intently, but the others with him had stopped and were watching my unsteady approach.

He looked up suddenly, seeing me standing over him. His words trailed off like tiny bubbles rising to the surface of water.

"My brother is dead and it does not mean nothing," I told him furiously, nails biting into the palms of my hands.

The man inhaled, wordless.

I grabbed the amber-colored drink in front of him and emptied it into his lap. When I fled outside, I realized that I had forgotten my coat and was still holding the glass. Turning to run, I let it go and it shattered on the cobblestones.

I climbed the street to the Upper Town, passing the lit candles of Stone Gate. I was aware of people praying in the few wooden pews. The stone inscriptions of the faithful which line the old gate flew past me. I can remember praying there as a child. And then again later, when my mother telephoned with the news that Željko was dead. Too late. I had asked the Virgin to intercede, for some kind of miracle. She was the same Virgin who now watched me from her portrait in the shrine. I could feel the sad eyes at my back, watching me pass through the gate.

He caught up with me on Strossmayer's Promenade above the city. I had heard him calling after me, but thought that he would merely fade away, persistence ultimately giving way to embarrassment. But as I sat down on one of the benches, shivering, he reached me and I saw with some surprise that he was holding my coat.

"Your friend said your name was Maja." He stood awkwardly a moment, breathing hard. His breath rose in puffs of frozen vapor and he sat abruptly on the bench beside me. "I'm sorry, Maja."

I started to cry, the palms of my hands pressed into the hollows of my eyes. He draped the coat around me. "I'm sorry, Maja," he repeated, putting an arm around me in an awkward embrace and resting a chin on the top of my head.

I remember wondering if I should push him away.

Later, when people asked how we met, we would look at one another with sheepish grins and then away.

But as we sat on the cold stone bench, his eyes filled with a viscous substance, some concentrate of tears. He told me that he was an old wolf, scarred and battered, that in his heart of hearts he had meant none of those things. Of course it was not for nothing.

It takes hours to reach Dubrovnik on the bus, and we arrive in early morning darkness. The approach to the city seems endless as we swing around first one bay and then another. A ferry idles in the inky water beside the Jadrolinija station, the garish shine of its lights filling the bus and rousing the last sleeping passengers, who shift with groans.

I know that we make one more turn to the bus station and then we swing into the parking lot. A drunken old man stands at the entrance like a sentry, muttering something and lifting a paper bag as a salute. When the doors open, cool morning air floods the airtight cavity in which we have been traveling, and we all lean semiconsciously toward it.

Somewhere around Split, a girl replaced the old woman next to me, and I see her disembark into the embrace of her boyfriend. *An engineer*, she explained at a rest stop, *with an amazing sex drive*. Someone is lending them an apartment for a long weekend away from her neighborhood, where no one minds his own business and everyone talks. It is her intention, she told me with a wink, to go home with a smile on her face.

"Are you meeting someone?" she asked.

"Yes," I lied with smooth efficiency. "My brother is on leave."
It was the first thing that came to mind.

She nodded. Then, after a moment, "He's lucky he didn't get
called up until now. My boyfriend's cousin lost both his legs behind Dubrovnik."

In the station, I watch the girl walk away arm in arm with her
boyfriend, who has taken her bag in his free hand. She looks back at
me only once with a quick wave of her hand. I drop onto a bench
beside the ticket window. Soon everyone has departed into the
predawn, and there is no one else on the platform except for the
woman in the ticket booth, who ignores me and reads a magazine.

The drunk who had stood at the entrance to the parking lot is
making painstaking progress toward the station. I watch as he
takes a few steps, stops, and speaks with first one invisible inter-
locutor and then another.

He makes a weaving beeline for me on the bench. Under the
platform lights I can see that he is an old man with greasy hair and
skin like leather. I am curious to hear what he will say.

"What are *you* doing here?" he asks in an accusatory voice.

"Vacation," I tell him, folding my hands primly in my lap. "I'm
here to meet my boyfriend, and I refuse to go home until there's a
smile on my face."

He looks at me a moment with a shrug and then shuffles off.

During the last days with Luka the snow had fallen for hours. It
piled thickly against the sides of his weekend house, and I stood at
the window watching it fall, a smoky blanket over my shoulders as
he loaded the woodstove behind me.

White flew from the sky in a cloud so thick I could not see the trees that were mere steps from the window. It was blowing in alternate directions so that for a moment it appeared to be falling upward, as if the ground was shedding its blanket into the white, discolored sky.

The snow threw back the light from the house. Before I turned from the window, I thought for a split second that I had seen my reflection in that snow, some hologram of self on the white storm, and not just the hollow-cheeked reflection in the window glass. But when I looked again the ice-woman was gone, and the snow was once more falling vertically from the sky.

Luka was saying something behind me. He had been irritable lately and argued about everything: I was late returning from work, I was growing too thin, I was mispronouncing the German word *München*. He was being ridiculous, but I admitted defeat each time, sensing his anger building toward something. The last time he had erupted, I had not seen him for a month. And then, unexpectedly, he had called me at three one morning from Stockholm, his voice thick with tears.

Coming to the weekend house had been his idea. "Please, Maja, there's no one with whom I'd rather be snowed in," he had told me. "I want to get out of the city and it will give us a chance to talk about things."

He was good for the first day, officiously wrapping me in a woolen blanket and bringing wood from the storeroom for the fire. But by the second day he had grown nervous, lighting one cigarette after another on the couch beside me.

Still another day went by, the snow slowing but continuing to shake itself out over the fields, and he had begun to pace while I tried to read a book. A few hours later, he began to rummage through the cabinets in the kitchen and returned with a half bottle of *lozavača*.

"Damn it, Luka!" I threw down my book.

"Stop it," he told me, and poured out a glass for himself.

"Stop what?"

"That look on your face."

"We haven't talked." I felt the tears biting into my words. "You said we would talk about things, and we haven't."

I sat in a silent rage on the couch as he drank three glasses and then sank down beside me, burrowing under the blanket covering my knees so that his head lay in my lap.

"We can talk if you want," he told me thickly. "Shall we discuss the weather or the state of the economy?" Even though he was tired and drunk, his voice kept its edge.

"Why are you doing this?"

I could feel the muscles in his neck stiffen.

"Let's talk about the war," I continued.

And he groaned. "Not again, Maja. Leave it alone."

I could feel his exhalations become even and the weight of his head change somehow, shifting so that I thought him asleep. It was then that I started to cry in earnest. When I managed to tamp the flow of tears, swiping my face with one hand, I realized that he was watching me, his eyes wide open and his expression unreadable.

"I can't give him back to you, Maja," he told me in a voice without inflection. "He's gone."

While Luka dug out the car the following day, the snow began to fall again. I stood at the window watching as he removed the ice from the windshield and dug a path down to the road. The plows had been out in the night, he told me that morning. He had heard them on the road below.

"Aren't you glad?" he asked me bitterly.

I was but said nothing.

He wore no hat as he shoveled, and the snow filled his black hair, muting its color and giving him the appearance of advanced age.

When I stepped through the door, shutting it behind me with a hollow sound, the cold was a relief after days inside. I closed my eyes and let the flakes melt against the heat of my face.

As soon as he had finished digging out a path, we filled the trunk with our luggage. Luka's tires were worn and he started to drive slowly.

"You can't wait to get rid of me," he said, hunched over the steering wheel. "All weekend you were fucking catatonic." I did not respond, and my silence infuriated him more than my screaming would have. He sped up and the windshield wipers could not keep up with the downpour of dry snow.

"There's someone else, isn't there?"

"Stop it, Luka!" I shouted, hitting the dashboard with my gloved hand.

He grabbed me by the back of my head, fingers twining for a moment almost lovingly through my hair. He made a move as if to push me face-first into the passenger window. I imagined the hard glass moving fast toward me and closed my eyes. But at the last second he let go of me so that my right cheek only grazed the window.

Something in Luka's eyes shifted and he lifted his hand apologetically, as if to stroke my tearstained cheek. When the real impact came, the dark shape running toward us with dizzying speed, I saw it flicker once against the windshield. Luka went to grab the steering wheel with both hands, and I fell forward, my head hitting the dashboard. It felt as if a river of blood started from my eyes, and I followed its warm path, allowing myself to float down it into darkness.

When I resurfaced, it was to the sound of windshield wipers, still moving to push the huge flakes away. My window was cracked into the shape of a spider's web and blood was at the center, like a family of shiny-backed ladybugs. The driver's side was ajar and I shivered, pushing my own side open, feeling as if I was pushing against a wall before falling out into a pile of snow.

"Luka," I called. The snow muted my voice.

He lay between the car and the fallen deer, his arms thrown out around it. I was struck for a moment by the absurd thought that he liked to lie that way with me in bed, cradling me to his chest. The deer was bleeding, turning the snow to red slush.

"Luka!" This time I screamed, the sound piercing the snow. He did not move.

Steam rose from the blood-soaked pieces of the deer's skin but not from Luka's breath. I made sure of this before turning and stumbling away.

I am almost there.

How does one thing become the other? They have become twins in my memory. I remember learning in high school about Janus, the double-faced Roman household god. I am left with nothing but an imaginary sentry who bears both men's faces.

The cuts on my face have faded to tiny lines. I am adept at smoothing them over with tinted creams, and people rarely comment on them anymore. It is only when I grow angry or upset that they turn red, lighting up like strands of vermilion glass. When I awake suddenly in the middle of the night, the marks on my face glow like embers buried under ash.

After the accident eight months ago, the first thing I did after returning to my Zagreb apartment was wash the blood from my face. The second was strip the bed, carrying the sheets in a bundle so that no evidence of Luka, no eyelash or sliver of fingernail, would remain. I sat on the bathroom floor, watching my reflection in the washing machine's circular glass door. Like a traveler pressing my face to a ship's submerged porthole, I watched the last traces of him dissolve in the soapy water and eject through the plastic tubing when the machine drained at the end of its cycle. But the name I muttered like a mantra into my hands was not my lover's. It was winter then.

At the station, I catch another local bus. There are no buses to the peak where my brother died. I know this because my brother's friend had explained it. They had gone up a month ago and laid a wreath on the spot. It had taken a rusty Fiat and an uphill hike. They had snapped photographs.

I have a choice now. I can try to get as close as I can or pick another destination.

An empty bus rolls into the station and a card beneath the windshield indicates that it is going southward to Cavtat. I do not hesitate and climb aboard. I pick a seat in the front and on the right, near the driver. As the bus starts I close my eyes and feel its movement shaking in every cell of my body.

The driver sees me in his rearview mirror. "Don't fall asleep yet," he tells me with a laugh. He is talkative, bored on his early morning route. "You're not from here."

I open my eyes, watching the city beyond the window. "No."

"Well, you've got to stay awake for the view."

The bus climbs out of the city. It groans with the effort and I feel like I am in an airplane that shudders into the sky. I am confused, wondering why we are rising up and away from the sea. For a moment I consider the illogical notion that this man has been sent to take me to the peak after all, but then I see the highway in front of us, how it drops back down in the distance. I had completely forgotten this road from our childhood trips.

"There!" the driver shouts, startling me. He slows the bus. "Not a more beautiful sight in the entire world."

And I look to my right, down to the walled, pearl-like city of Dubrovnik, past it to Fort Lovrijenac, from whose heights lovers have been known to throw themselves to their deaths. The dawn has made the sea silver and smooth as a looking glass.

"It will be beautiful for you today," the driver is saying, changing the station on the radio.

My brother died in full view of the sea.

I step down from the bus into the still-sleeping seaside town of Cavtat. The bus departs behind me with a roar and I stand beneath some trees, across from the *riva* where Željko and I had walked as children. The sun is rising higher and there are actual circles of light that fall on the sidewalk between the leaves of trees. I step into one of them now and the warmth veils my skin. I feel its kiss on the back of my head.

There is a headland that I remember past the *riva*. It lies beneath the Old Graveyard, and we had swum from its rocks. I cover the distance quickly. No one sees me as I traverse the *riva* from one end to the other, and I strike out on the sea path at the end of it.

Željko, I say to the air on my right. *Luka*, I tell the left. I squeeze both hands as if they are holding something. We are a strange trio.

My brother would grow brown on our visits here. I merely freckled, my paleness gazing from beneath the shade of pines. Our mother could identify us when we swam underwater, a dark shape and a light shape, making faces at one another so that we laughed without sound, a roar of bubbles exploding against the surface.

I walk toward a dilapidated stone house at the tip of the headland and past it, down onto a field of sloping rocks and wading pools. At the edge, where the sea begins, I select a spot and stand looking down.

There is a storm of movement coming from beneath: rapid schools of metallic fish, corals, and sea grass that sways in every current, a host of dark and unidentifiable shadows.

When I dive, the air whines past my ears and I plummet past the startled fish and seaweed. I swim as far out as I can, my lungs constricting, and then surface. I turn so that my back is to the hillside and watch white sails heading seaward. There is a low sound that has started in my ears, two voices in discussion over my bent head, and I think for a moment how easy it would be to join them. I could just close my eyes. It would be the most logical move I have made in months. I tread water for a moment, and then swim back.

Stillness

THE CITY IS FADING. I chart its decline from a cellar with damp walls and a concrete floor. It does not make the sound of an eraser against paper, the soft rubbing that produces worn white space and gray crumbs of what formerly was. But the shelling has the same effect. Seated on the mattress which leaked ash-colored stuffing and dust as I dragged it down the steps in the first days of the siege, I can hear the city bending into nothing.

Sometimes the shelling shakes plaster from the ceiling. The colorless powder hangs in the air for a long while before settling in a gritty blanket on the floor. I have swept it into corners, where it is already ankle deep, and coughed its sharp grit into my handkerchief.

The dust will soon cover everything and I panic, imagining it flooding the whole cellar. In fact, I know that all the plaster in the building could not fill it entirely. Perhaps only an Orkan rocket could do the job, bringing floors, sinks, and furniture down on top of me. But I can hardly breathe when I imagine it, when I imagine suffocating in a sea of dust. It will fill my nose and ears, drowning me. And I will disappear like the city.

O Vukovar, I write on scraps of paper by the cellar's single window. It is high up, and at one time I could see the feet of people walking by. Now there are no pedestrians, only an occasional voice, frantic and disembodied. Sandbags are piled against the window, except for one corner which admits a hesitant glow. I have a handful of candles left, but am trying to conserve them. I had an oil lamp, but its fuel and the batteries in the flashlight are already spent.

Sometimes I write in complete darkness, strange sloping lines and wandering letters, words barely decipherable come morning. I write as if writing verse to a woman. *O city of my birth.*

The clean lines of your buildings, the pavement of your streets, are nothing more than splinters and craters where streets once lived. Your two rivers have become the entrance to the underworld, your water tower a pocked gravestone.

I stole up once at dusk to see proof of it, and it is true. With each passing day you disappear more. Aboveground nothing moves except the bombs, which descend, and the smoke, which rises into a steel-colored sky. Bodies lie everywhere because there is no opportunity to bury them. Several have been killed trying.

I myself saw a lone pair of legs standing upright in their boots, no body left to identify their owner. They startled me at first, because in the gloom I mistook them for a man standing quietly and watching me. I started, not having seen another living person for days, then realized that it was no man, only his residue shot through with bone. The dark buildings stood around us at attention, and I paused for a dumb moment, thinking of scissors cutting at memory.

In the end, it is only the underground that exists, the thousands of beating hearts in confined spaces. I lay down on the unrecognizable sidewalk outside my building, the silent legs my only witness, and placed an ear to the ground and heard them past the shells and shouts in the distance. I heard the drumbeats of all those buried people, of a city living underground. And it was the only thing that made me rise to my feet and descend once more into the darkness. Even as the city sinks, its walls razed to nothing, our breath holds it up. Stubborn survival is our only rebellion.

In the city above, nothing living moves. Only the clouds in the sky and, one would guess, the moon. *O Vukovar. You live though you are ground to dust.*

I was a writer once, although I do not remember whether I wrote fiction or fact. Perhaps I was a journalist for a newspaper, charting economic trends. Or maybe I wrote carefree lines that earned me awards and praise. It seems unimportant now, although I cannot help thinking of the luxury of those days, the luxury of saying little. (I am convinced that I said little.) I had a name, but have misplaced it now. I had an entire history, once. A wife, children perhaps, but in the cellar I am alone.

The hands that move in the gloom belong to an old man, and I have no mirror in which to examine my face. I do not care and am sure that, whatever its reflection, it would only shock me and plunge me into misery.

I recognize myself only as the shadow that moves between the downpours of plaster. I believe that toxic rain has bleached me to the color of papery nothing. But still I write. On discarded labels from cans, on old newspapers, on the ripped-out pages of books. My pen runs out of ink, and I search out another. I push my hands into all the cobwebbed spaces, thinking of fat, happy days in which one would not pursue a lowly pen dropped into the musty dark. In the end, I find the snapped half of a pencil. I carve its tip carefully with my knife, feeling the oily graphite between thumb and forefinger. The pencil makes a scratching sound against the paper, and when I am done I fold it into a square like all the others.

I open the window the inch that it will go and push the paper out with my fingers. It flutters briefly at the end of my hand, and I concentrate on that last instant of contact until the wind takes it, until the city accepts it into her dark and shattered heart.

I think, *My only present to you.*

I remember that I was not always alone here. I ran into the cellar when the airplanes began their strafing and tanks fired on the city, and I remember the push and pull of other panicked bodies in the stairwell. I seem to recall a shifting population in those first few days. Someone gave me a blanket, and I shared my mattress with a dying woman. There was also a young woman with two sons. The dying woman's groans finally drove me to one of the darker corners of the cellar where my teeth hammered in my skull. By the time I returned, she was dead, and we carried her body up into the courtyard. The city's defenders helped us with the burial, placing her in a crater conveniently carved by a shell. We covered her with chips of exploded pavement, roof tiles, and broken glass. I think that I uprooted weeds growing miraculously in one corner and added them for good measure, in order to soften the harsh geometry of her burial. When I returned to the cellar, I saw that she had left an oblong stain of blood on the mattress.

Our small group was silent after the burial, but then began playing guessing and word games to pass the time. The elder of the two boys had a transistor radio and we listened to reports from the outside world, to voices transmitted from our own city. "Vukovar is bleeding," a man's voice implored citizens of the still-living world. "We don't know how much longer we can stand."

As the batteries weakened, the announcer's voice grew fainter, until it was overtaken by white noise and then silence. The elder son had large black eyes that I could sense even in the dark. They were like pitch in the dark well of that chamber. On the cusp of manhood, he was already conscious of its demands, and tried to conceal his fear from the rest of us.

The younger boy had a birthday that first month, so it occurs to me that we must have been counting days then. The night before, his mother had stolen upstairs while they slept, and the cellar echoed with the sound of shelling. I had pleaded with her not to go, but she shook me off and fled up the stairs. The building had already been hit a number of times, and we hardly knew if it still existed above us. I imagined her emerging from the cellar door into a vast desert, but then I heard her movements on the floors above and her footsteps dislodged a fine cascade of plaster. It fell on the faces of her sleeping sons, but did not wake them. I looked at them, my heart in my mouth through all those minutes. What would I do if she did not return?

But soon I heard her steps on the stairs and she reappeared, carrying armfuls of toys and books. She had even managed to scrounge more food and batteries. She replaced the spent ones in the radio, and it rose from the dead for one precious week more. When the boys awoke, they were greeted in the half-light by those articles of their appropriated childhood, arranged in a semicircle on the floor.

"Happy birthday!" She kissed her younger son and then the older. She handed me a book of poetry that she had managed to salvage and shoved in her pocket. As the boys crowed happily over their toys, I retired to the faint light by the window and began to read. In the weeks that followed, I tore out page after page and filled them with my frantic penmanship, sacrificing those thin husks for my present circumstances.

Naturally, the woman and her children disappeared as well.

The younger son became ill and lay on the mattress for two days with a fever. It may have been the lack of fresh air, or the scarcity of food. We scrounged what we could, but there was no meat, no milk, no fruit. Or maybe it was the water, which had been the first casualty of war. We had drained all the radiators in the building, but the water was gritty and tasted of metal.

The boy tossed from side to side on his mattress, and his mother, brother, and I kept vigil. But the fever only crept higher, and with no thermometer to gauge it we pressed the flats of our hands against his forehead. On the third night, she left him bundled in blankets and went up to the street for help. The shelling seemed suddenly less. I do not know how long she wandered, how long his older brother and I listened to the labored breathing, imagining the damage being wrought inside his head.

She had found two young men from the city's defense. Scarcely more than boys themselves, they would help get her son to the hospital, and I realized that she expected all of us to leave together.

"Please," the older boy urged me. He pulled at my hand, but I would not be led.

"Come with us," his mother begged. "We'll be safer at the hospital."

But I could not leave the cellar and shook my head. I was suddenly frightened, more frightened than I had ever been. My legs would not function properly, and my heart raced. The two young men were anxious. "We've got to go now," one of them told her. "Before it gets light and the shelling starts again."

They began carrying the boy up the stairs, and she pushed her other son in front of her.

She had insisted on keeping the cellar lit during her son's illness, and we had gone through much of our supply of candles. In the yellow light her face retracted, and I felt a sudden tenderness for its shadows.

"Please, come with us," she said again, but I smiled at her, shaking my head a second time. I turned her gently and kept my hand at her elbow on the first few steps.

Five minutes after they left, the bombing began again, heavier than any we had yet seen. I imagined them making their way between the falling shells, between the incendiary devices. I willed their safe passage but do not know whether they made it in the end, or whether the little boy survived. I sat for some time in the light of that candle, until it burned its way down to the puddle of wax and vanished with a sigh.

———

At night the city breathes. Sometimes I tap on pipes with a piece of broken cinder block. Sometimes people in the other cellars tap back. In the army I had been a telegraphist. I am amazed that I remember the codes but not my name. I tap out messages for amusement.

It is a day in autumn, I state.

The next night I ask no one in particular, *Are you there?*

On the third I quote Ujević's "Notturno," although I am far from the passion of youth. *Tonight, I will die from beauty.* Then I remember another line toward the end of the poem. *Let us weep, weep in silence*, I tell the pipes, leaning my forehead against them.

And someone answers, the tapping so faint that I can hardly make out the words. But I do, and their sorrowful message brings a smile to my face. *Let us die, die alone.*

For a moment I think it is that long-dead poet speaking to me. Who knows, I think in a moment of recklessness, maybe he has been hiding in Vukovar's cellars all these years, watching the seasons of sunlight and frost from the grave with one window.

I write the pencil down. I squeeze all life from it. In the end, it writes no more and I am left scrabbling through plaster that reaches my shins. My fishing expedition yields nothing but a piece of wire, and I move it against a scrap of old wallpaper whose pattern had, in the light of day, teased a whisper of memory in me but in the end drawn no concrete recollection. I move it against the yellowed back, flaking with some ancient glue. I move it and will it to write, to produce a rusted but legible alphabet.

In the morning I fold it with my eyes closed, not daring to look and see if my nighttime efforts have brought any reward. I fold this one tighter than the others, and push it into the street.

The shelling stops. Weeks have passed, perhaps months. Sun-starved, we rise out of the ground like fog. We clamber from our hiding places, from hip-deep dust, into an overcast autumn day. The sun does not emerge with us. It is hiding yet in the cellars, perhaps not having heard the orders to give up the ground.

"Eighty-six days," an old woman with a shuttered face whispers to me, and I shake my head slowly from side to side. I can imagine her counting them out with teeth thrown into an old pot.

Women come up into the air, ashen-faced, holding the hands of their children. I see a small girl of about seven whose hair has gone completely silver. She is solemn and holds a stuffed animal in her hand. Upon closer inspection I see that it is an eyeless dog, with hanging threads where black buttons had once been sewn. Her head shines like a torch and I follow her on the road that leads out of the city.

I look for the woman with her two sons, but do not see her. I look also for the woman we buried, imagining her labored gait on the road out of the city. I wonder which of the faces is my fellow pipe-tapper.

There are women with infants on their hips and I stare, shuddering at the thought of a population born in the ground.

A man comes up to me and grasps my arm. He says my name, but as soon as he speaks it, I forget it again and we are separated. The letters rise in the vertical smoke over the city. I am more comfortable without them.

Behind us stand the soldiers, and the irregulars with their overgrown beards and wild eyes. When they smile, they reveal jagged teeth. Their breath is contagion to my city and I feel myself go pale. Paler than plaster, and paler even than the children disfigured by the dark.

I raise a fist at them and shout. I use language they understand, harsh vernacular. I do not bother with literary devices, or well-crafted sentences or metaphors. Subtlety is wasted on them. At first they are only amused by the screaming old man. They move against me as a wall and push me into the ground with their guns and laugh. I scrabble in the dirt, bringing up cold handfuls of shrapnel, tile, and bone, which I throw at them. "That's all you deserve of her!" I scream.

A woman passing in the road starts to weep, and it occurs to me that I once knew her. *Wife*, I want to call after her. *Daughter*. But then she, too, fades into the throng.

The soldiers have become enraged. They pluck me up as if I were weightless. They tell me they will snap my bones, but my taunts are without end. I curse their fathers and their uncles. I curse their children, born and yet to be. I curse their mothers. Oh, their wicked, wicked mothers.

And I am disappearing, like my city. I am fading into the overcast sky. Dust of me scatters in the street and through still, silent gutters. Dust rises in the air and becomes entrapped in the feathers of a wheeling bird, which has suddenly reappeared after the months of shelling. And from his wings I see my city. It is borne out on her residents' backs. Its breath occupies their lungs and they turn their eyes upward to me. I am shaken from the sky, from the churning wings. I come to rest in her silent shell. *O Vukovar, beloved. My burial ground.*

Acknowledgments

MANY THANKS go to my mother and father, who not only under-stood my restless nature but let me wander. They have been my best teachers, and provided outstanding advice on countless drafts of these stories. To my brother, Andrew, for his inherent decency, and to my Aunt Katja and Aunt Iva, the embodiment of how we endure. To my friends for their support: the Forssen family, Judy and Milan Brozovic, Katherine Rosich and family, Laura Sims, my fellow Hague BCSers. To Jennie Page for her valuable feedback and help in finding a writing space. I am indebted to Melissa Hammerle and New York University's Creative Writing

ACKNOWLEDGMENTS

Program, to the New York Times Company Foundation, and to the Fulbright Program. To Breyten Breytenbach, Stuart Dybek, and Nicholas Christopher for crucial support and guidance. To my editor, Ethan Nosowsky, whose astute comments helped me look at these pages with fresh eyes. And to my agent, Sandra Dijkstra, whose faith in my work was unwavering.